PRAISE FOR

PEST

"Wry, funny, and full of heart, *Pest* takes you on a nimble-footed tour of Santa Barbara's 'dark side,' while remaining true to its coming-of-age roots. Recommended for readers who like their teen angst leavened with laughs."

—Bruce Hale, bestselling author of *The Chet Gecko Mysteries* and *Clark the Shark*

"Elizabeth Foscue's coming-of age tale simply oozes charm. Locals will instantly recognize the incredibly detailed look at life in Santa Barbara (boy, you just can't believe how accurate!), and all will be equally captivated by *Pest's* Hal, and her spirited nature."

—Valerie R. Rice, Author of *Lush Life: Food & Drinks from the Garden*

"In *Pest*, Elizabeth Foscue portrays an insidiously wealthy enclave, crawling with teen drama and teeming with unwanted legged creatures lurking inside mansion walls. Working for her family's pest control business, Hallie Mayhew drives a spider topped vehicle as the perfect analogy for the pesky hormonal life of a high schooler ruled by uncomfortable, itchy peer encounters that lurk, irk—and elude. Ripe with socio-economic rifts and teen angst, the misunderstood girl next door, Hallie, presents a unique 'most likely to succeed' protagonist who isn't afraid to face the task of college applications—or pick up dead critters along the way. A YA read that is both entertaining and intriguing."

—Liz Ruckdeschel, author of the *What If...* series

PEST

PEST

ELIZABETH FOSCUE

KEYLIGHT
BOOKS

Keylight Books
an imprint of Turner Publishing Company
Nashville, Tennessee

www.turnerpublishing.com

Pest

Cover Artwork by Nicole Rifkin
Cover Design by Mallory Grigg
Book Design by Mallory Collins

Library of Congress Cataloging-in-Publication Data

Names: Foscue, Elizabeth, author.
Title: Pest / by Elizabeth Foscue.
Description: Nashville, Tennessee : Keylight Books, [2022] | Audience: Ages 12-14. | Audience: Grades 7-9. |
    Identifiers: LCCN 2021030596 (print) | LCCN 2021030597 (ebook) | ISBN 9781684428120 (paperback) | ISBN 9781684428137 (hardcover) | ISBN 9781684428144 (ebook)
Subjects: CYAC: Pests--Control--Fiction. | Family-owned business enterprises--Fiction. | High schools--Fiction. | Schools--Fiction. | Santa Barbara (Calif.)--Fiction. | LCGFT: Novels.
Classification: LCC PZ7.1.F6715 Pe 2022 (print) | LCC PZ7.1.F6715 (ebook) | DDC [Fic]--dc23
LC record available at https://lccn.loc.gov/2021030596
LC ebook record available at https://lccn.loc.gov/2021030597

Printed in the United States of America

For Hank Foscue, who taught me to love a good story.

CHAPTER 1

Rats," I said.

"What? No. Are you sure?"

It was the last day of August and the Montecito morning was almost warm. The soothing tinkle of a water feature screened the ambient sounds of lawnmowers and leaf blowers. The sky was blue and clear and the air smelled of flowering jasmine.

I stared down at the field of scattered rat poo. "Yes."

Irma, the house manager, said some very bad words in Spanish and stomped back and forth across a patch of wooly thyme. The chateau-style Montecito estate had been recently landscaped, the guest cottage planted with a thoughtful mix of drought-tolerant succulents and a ground cover of flowering ice plant.

Rats love ice plant.

"How did they get in?" Irma wailed. "No, it doesn't matter. You have to get them out. The Guests,"—she referred to them with verbal capitals—"say the noise kept them up all night long."

This I did not doubt. The rustic plaster application on the exterior walls camouflaged the telltale rat smudges, but to a trained eye—which, I'm sad to say, mine is—they were everywhere. And the rat runways, those little trails rats bushwhack as they go about their ratty business, were spacious boulevards.

This place had serious numbers of rats in the ceiling and anyone staying here would be getting an all-night, all-rat revue.

"We'll have to tent it," I said.

"What?" Irma looked like she might have a stroke. "No! Where will The Guests go?"

There must have been ten bedrooms in the enormous house I'd passed in my search for the service lot, but maybe sharing a roof with visitors was considered gauche, maybe the main house had bad feng shui, maybe the guests were Suppressive Persons—I didn't even ask. Rich Montecito weirdos make all other rich weirdos look like amateurs.

"Can't you just block up the hole? Trap them in there?" Irma pleaded.

Trapped rats are cannibalistic. If you seal them up together, your rat-Broadway becomes the rat-Octagon as they fight and scream and consume one another. But this is way more detail than most clients want. I gave an apologetic shrug and pulled the metal clipboard from under my arm, turning to a fresh estimate form.

"Oh my god, oh my god. Listen, okay? We can tent it if you're done by four. The Guests are wine-tasting in Santa Ynez but they'll be back for dinner."

Clients always want the job done by four, if not immediately. And, as my dad likes to say, if wishes had wings, bullfrogs wouldn't bump their butts jumping over logs.

I wrote a nice, big number at the bottom of the form, ripped the sheet off the pad, and handed it over. "The structure will have to be vacated for seventy-two hours. And we can't get to it before Thursday." I turned and padded over to the path I'd walked in on. If there was any traffic on the 101, I was going to be late. "Call that number if you want to get on the schedule."

"Wait!" Irma shook the estimate at me. "Where are you going?"

I answered without looking back as I hurried in the direction of the service lot. "School."

The 101 northbound was clear and I pulled into the lot of my high school with two minutes to spare, both of which I burned finding a space big enough for my truck. Ford Rangers aren't much bigger than your average compact car but the giant black spider mounted to the driver's side of mine complicates parking. As gimmicks go, it's extremely effective. My dad's pest control company is the largest in Santa Barbara County and much of the credit goes to the fleet of white work trucks zipping around town under attack by giant spiders. I call my spider Shelob because she's a demon to park and her job is to guard the truck.

I found a spot in the very back of the lot, to the left of a shiny gray Tesla Model S that had been parked diagonally across two spaces. All that extra space was perfect for Shelob. I backed in and hoped the Tesla driver didn't need to leave before me, or he'd be crawling across from the passenger side. I pulled off the blue Mayhew Pest Control polo I'd been wearing over my t-shirt, shrugged on the straps of my backpack, and headed toward the main building.

Santa Barbara High School (est. 1875) might be the loveliest public high school campus in the country. Not that I've seen them all, but this one is ludicrously beautiful. Wide lawns and nineteenth-century Spanish-style buildings sprawl across forty acres in the city's pricey Upper East neighborhood. Movies have been filmed here. It's beyond gorgeous. Unfortunately, it's still high school.

A white Chevy Tahoe made a screeching turn into the parking spot directly in front of me. I glanced down to make sure all my toes were still represented in three dimensions as the passenger door opened and a tiny red-haired girl tumbled out, gasping my name.

"Hal! Ohhhhhhhh my god, we missed you!"

They'd seen me yesterday. They live across the street.

The driver's side door opened and an incrementally taller red-haired girl stepped down, yawning. "Hi, Hal."

Montana and Madison Forbes look as alike as any siblings in existence with their oval faces, tiny frames, and long, straight hair. They're both dancers, so they tend to dress similarly, and they both share the fervent conviction that a ponytail without a ribbon tied around it is an abomination. More than one new student has mistaken them for twins.

People who know them don't make that mistake. For one thing, Madison is fourteen months younger and a junior. For another, the blood in her veins is one hundred percent serotonin. She doesn't walk, she bounces. Her sentences begin with squeals and end with exclamation points. Whenever confused classmates ask, I advise them that Madison is the one who acts like she's on her way home from a unicorn rave.

Montana, on the other hand, can be fierce and focused but generally keeps things pretty low-key. Except when she's driving. When she's driving, you can kind of see where Madison gets it.

"Can you believe we're driving!?" Madison squealed.

"Driving your mom's car," I observed. This was something Montana had sworn never to do.

Montana made a face. "She says she's done driving us now that I have a license and she's only buying me a car if we re-join dance team. So. I guess we'll be driving the Dance Mom-mobile for the foreseeable future."

We all paused to take in the back of the enormous SUV. A chrome frame engraved "♥Mommy's M&M's: Montana and Madison♥" bracketed the license plate and a pink stick-figure family of four clasped hands across the rear window.

"Whatever," Montana said dismissively. "We're done with those salad-obsessed, backstabbing glitter-sniffers."

Madison seconded, "We wouldn't come back if they begged us."

"Which they totally will," her sister predicted, crossing her arms. "I don't care. Mom can suck it."

I raised my eyebrows. Not that I disagreed with the sentiment, but no one—especially her daughters—told Mrs. Forbes to suck it. Not to her face, anyway.

"So, what are you doing after school?" Montana asked me. "For the first time in human history, we don't have practice. Should we hang out?"

I checked the calendar on my phone—only out of habit, because it always says the same thing—and shook my head. "I've gotta work. What about lunch?" As upperclassmen, we can leave campus for lunch, and there are plenty of tasty options within quick walking distance.

Montana opened her mouth to answer then shut it as Madison jerked to a halt beside her. I dodged sideways so I wouldn't run her down and stumbled over an abandoned kombucha bottle, which my foot launched across the asphalt before landing in the puddle of spillage.

"What is *she* doing here?" Madison said, her eyes wide as she stared across the lot.

In an exercise of well-bred subtlety, Montana and I wheeled around and stared at the girl climbing out of a small Mercedes SUV. Shiny, light brown hair in a high ponytail. Pretty. I didn't recall seeing her before but there were twenty-two hundred people at our school, so that didn't count for much. I shook kombucha off my Vans and bent to pick up the glass bottle before someone ran it over.

"Unbelievable," Montana hissed. "They already replaced me."

"What?" I had obviously missed something.

"That's Britta. She's the top veteran dancer at Dos Pueblos. They must have promised her Captain to get her to transfer here," she said darkly.

Madison looked uncertain. "Maybe she's just visiting."

Montana nodded slowly and said, "Maybe she's just handing out free puppies."

Madison's face lit with interest.

"No," Montana said sternly. "There are no puppies. She's here for dance team."

I paused by the trash bin—we have three different kinds of recycling plus green waste; it always takes me a minute to decode the options—and they kept going, Montana muttering furiously as they stalked off in the direction of Building D.

Oh, good. Lunch should be pleasant.

My first class, AP American History, was in Building A. The late bell rang just as I entered the arched breezeway and I had to duck into the bathroom to avoid Mrs. Perz, the Dean of Students.

Mrs. Perz had cornered me the very first day of school to hassle me about my arrival time. It's true that some mornings . . . well, most mornings . . . okay, fine, *all* mornings, I am very slightly late for school. During the school year, my dad's office manager tends to schedule me for early morning emergency calls. I think she feels like she needs to get some labor out of me since I squander seven hours a day at school. And, while my dad pays me decent money, I'm an hourly employee. I need the jobs. Anyway, it isn't like I'm behind the bleachers vaping, if that's really a thing people do, or obsessing over my hair. I'm *working.*

Mrs. Perz doesn't care. "Do you know how many times you were marked tardy last year, Miss Mayhew?" she'd asked, tapping her tablet against the side of her leg.

"Nineteen," I'd answered promptly, if not wisely.

Mrs. Perz's eyes had narrowed. "The Student Handbook specifies that any student who accrues twenty tardies in a school year shall be subject to attendance failure. And, do I need to remind you, this year ten tardies will get you an in-school suspension? I imagine most college admissions boards would find that disqualifying."

"Oh, wow, I didn't realize." I really hadn't. The ISS rule was new. Not good.

Mrs. Perz had faked a smile and promised, "I'll be watching you this year."

Just what I needed.

So this morning I put a little extra muscle in my hustle and made it from the bathroom to my first class a mere three minutes after the late bell. That was a cool four minutes before the teacher showed up, so all was well. I'd lucked out getting American History first period. Ms. Grijalva had started dating Coach Bell, the hot assistant football coach, sometime over the summer and they were still in Stage One: Lust. This was the third day of school and, so far, she'd rolled in at least five minutes late every day.

I don't play any sports but I know Coach Bell from freshman

Honors Geography. That was the year the veteran geography teacher had relocated for her husband's job a week before school started and Coach Bell, who'd just been hired, had been the only teacher available that period. It was quite a class. The standout was the unit on Australia, which Coach Bell spent discussing rabbit plagues, documented crocodile attacks, and the Great Barrier "wreath"—specifically how rad it would be to jet ski across it hunting sharks. I prayed it would take Ms. Grijalva at least until the end of the semester to realize he was an idiot. Or maybe she didn't care. He was pretty hot.

My phone buzzed in my lap as Ms. Grijalva started her lecture. I glanced down to see "Mom" on the lock screen and automatically hit "ignore." A minute later it buzzed again and I repeated the process. Then a third time.

Whoever invented voicemail obviously knew my mother. She can't remember schedules, can't conduct a phone conversation in less than twenty minutes, and seems to genuinely believe that, if you didn't answer the first time, you must not have heard the phone ringing. Don't misunderstand: I love my mom. She's nice. Very nice. Like an essential oil–slathered, yoga-obsessed Disney Princess. Her pond and koi service, Pond Guru, has all the biggest accounts in town because even the swans love her, and swans hate everybody. I can *almost* see how my dad fell for her, although I've always known him to be more practical than that. You don't have to be Dr. Phil to forecast disaster for the union of a woman who nurtures little creatures and a man who exterminates them.

They somehow made it to my ninth birthday before calling it quits. The divorce was emotional and nasty and the aftermath was an exhausting carnival of spite. Things haven't improved much. My mom takes every minute I spend working for Mayhew

Pest Control and every night I spend at my dad's house as a rejection of her love and values. My dad hates my mom's new husband and is still mad about the time I got salmonella poisoning helping her clean a turtle pond.

Ninety seconds after the third call, a text came through. WHERE ARE YOU PLEASE CALL ME. Sure. In the middle of class. I sighed and put my phone away in my bag.

At ten thirty, I had just pulled out my phone to text my mom back when a summons came from the college counselor. I signed out of study hall and reported to the administration building. For most twelfth graders, this would be their second or—in the case of extreme slackers—maybe even first college planning session. I, on the other hand, had been a regular visitor since freshman year. There was no room for error in my college campaign. I had put three long years of time and effort into this endeavor. I hadn't expected a meeting this morning, though. The pieces of my plan were in place and all that was left to do now was wait.

The engraved plastic door plate once read GUIDANCE but someone with Wite-Out and an axe to grind had changed it to RIDICULE. In the three years I'd been visiting this office, no effort had been made to clean or replace it, which pretty much tells you everything you need to know about Dr. McLoren, College Guidance Counselor.

Fortunately, he likes me.

"How's your mother?" he asked jovially as I settled myself into his visitor chair. Dr. McLoren is six-foot-four with thick gray hair and a matching mustache. His hobbies include reading the classics in their original dead languages, terrorizing college-bound seniors, and tenderly cultivating lotus plants in his home water garden. My mom has the maintenance contract for his koi, so he's aware she mostly exists on an alternate astral plane.

I spared a thought for my phone, which continued to blow up in my backpack. "Fine. How's the Parent's Night speech coming?" "Heh heh." He chuckled evilly. "I'm gonna burn down the barn. They'll be talking about it for years."

I had no doubt.

He took a sip of coffee from a mug that said, "Teaching high school is like being pecked to death by a duck," and got down to business. "So, in looking over your file, it occurs to me that you're a little light on extracurriculars."

"I have extracurriculars," I reminded him. "I have a full-time job and a part-time job. And an unpaid koi indenture."

He grimaced in acknowledgement.

"Oh, and Spanish club."

"Olé!" He leaned forward and ordered, "You let me know when it's sopapilla day."

"I'll bring you a plate," I promised.

He sat back in his chair and gave me a serious look. "Spanish club meets twice a year. You need to add something that attests to an outside interest, Hal. A club. A team. Even a hobby."

"A hobby," I repeated incredulously.

"I can get you on the Latin team. We went to state last year." I stared.

"No? I hear the dance team is holding tryouts. No, okay. Well," he paused, then offered doubtfully, "there's always the yearbook."

This wasn't making any sense to me. "You said my application looked great. You said my employment history spoke to my dedication and work ethic."

"It does, certainly it does," he assured me. "Your course rigor is outstanding and your test scores are exceptional. But the University of California system is going to look at your extracurriculars. And if you want to qualify for the SBCC Promise—"

SBCC Promise is a local non-profit that provides qualifying graduates of local high schools with two years of free tuition to Santa Barbara City College. Amazing program. For other people.

"Dr. McLoren." I laid my hands flat on his desk. "You are familiar with The Plan. You helped make The Plan." I waited for his nod, which came a bit slowly for my peace of mind, then stated, "Hobbies are not part of The Plan."

"I know, but the City College—"

I shook my head vigorously. "No, no. No City College. No UC schools." I twitched as an intense itching sensation shot up my spine. My dog was on a flea regimen but the *Pulex irritans* had been known to hang out in schools. I gave the industrial carpet beneath my chair a suspicious look but didn't see anything moving.

I transferred my suspicious look to Dr. McLoren. The thought of four more years in-state or, god forbid, in this town—it was enough to give me hives. I'd worked extra shifts for two years, saved every possible cent, all to cover the living expenses I would incur going to school far, far away from Santa Barbara. And every hour not spent earning had been dedicated to research and writing. I wasn't kidding around with this. California and I needed time apart. Years, actually. Maybe a lifetime of them.

I took a deep, calming breath. "You know I'm going to an East Coast school."

"I know that's what you want, Hal, but it's hard to predict what kind of financial aid packages you'll be offered, and the expense of going out-of-state is considerable."

I stared at him dumbly. We had this covered. In The Plan. Yes, East Coast schools were expensive but—a horrible thought hit like seagull poop. My eyes went wide. For a moment, my heart stopped. I formed my next words with numb lips. "Something's happened with the Verhaag Scholarship."

The Verhaag Scholarship was the crux of The Plan. The fund had been endowed by one of Santa Barbara's most prominent families in honor of Augusta Verhaag, their founding matriarch and—rumor had it—mistress/muse of famed Gold Rush-era poet Robert W. Service. Luckily for her descendants, Augusta had eventually given up pining for poets and married railroad tycoon Duke Verhaag, whose immense fortune enabled all subsequent crops of Verhaags to live the private club life in Montecito. Duke had been a pretty nasty character, however, and the Verhaags' preferred narrative attributed paternity of Augusta's only child, Angus, to Robert W. Service. They never came right out and *said* this, of course, because that would be a) tacky and b) easily disproven with a cheek swab from one of Service's legitimate— and very annoyed—descendants. Instead the Verhaags used the annual award ceremony to coyly imply to local news outlets that Service had, well, serviced their sainted grandmother, and at this point it was local lore, true or not.

They could imply their blood ran sourdough for all I cared. The award covered the full cost of tuition to the winner's choice of accredited college or university and I had plotted for the past three years to ensure this year, *I* would be the Santa Barbara High School student whose research paper was judged to "best honor the legacy of Robert W. Service and bring added depth and insight to our understanding of this gifted poet's life and oeuvre." For three years, I'd lived, breathed, and anxiety-induced insomnia'd Robert W. Service. At the risk of sounding over-confident, I had this in the bag.

Dr. McLoren looked deeply uncomfortable. "The Verhaag scholarship has a bit of a reputation for nepotism . . ."

I was aware. The *Santa Barbara News-Journal*, when not publishing editorial rants about "the illegals," loved to print stories about Verhaags throwing charity benefits, and Verhaags playing polo, and, of course, articles about the Verhaag Scholarship, which never failed to mention that it had been awarded on seven occasions to direct descendants of Augusta Verhaag. It was part of their legacy. Verhaags went to college on Verhaag scholarships. They didn't need the money but they sure did like to win stuff.

"But the winner has to be a student here," I reminded him, "and there aren't any Verhaags in my class."

"Well, as to that," Dr. McLoren said grimly, "I'm told we have a new dance team captain."

CHAPTER 2

So that was who the Dancing Dons imported to replace Montana. Britta *Verhaag*. I was suddenly less thrilled that Montana and Madison had kicked off their sequined shackles.

I must have looked pretty bad as I left Dr. McLoren's office. His next appointment, a girl from my English class, made a panicked sound and begged the receptionist to reschedule her. The school therapist, spying me through her open doorway, made sympathetic noises and tried to pull me into her lair. So not happening. Even in my current condition I knew better than to engage. She gave me the hard sell but I am a child of divorce and I know how to handle therapists. She eventually gave up, sending me on my way with a suicide prevention brochure and a Hershey's Kiss.

I popped the chocolate in my mouth and staggered out of the building, forgetting to ignore my phone when I felt it buzz again.

What, I typed back.

SOS! SAD EVENT AT ARCADA POND CAN YOU COVER. EMERGENCY!!!!!!

And so I found myself skipping out on my pleasant lunch plans to skim a dead fish out of a turtle pond.

La Arcada's turtle pond is actually a large fountain basin filled with rocks, turtles, and koi. It sits in the center of a small, elaborately tiled plaza, surrounded by an art gallery and three popular restaurants. The proximity of the restaurants is unfortunate for the resident koi, particularly Josephine's, a bakery and coffee shop that attracts lots of families with little kids. Little kids who like to stare at the turtles and share their muffins with the fishies.

I cruised up with a trash bag and a five gallon bucket, trying to look casual for the sake of the al fresco lunch crowd. Regrettably, someone—one of the restaurant managers or maybe the property manager—had done a very official-looking job of cordoning off the fountain with folding Wet Floor signs and orange hazard tape. As soon as I stepped over the tape, all eyes were on me.

I glanced down at the pond and groaned. Of course it would be that one. Most of the koi carp in this habitat were young and small, the exception being a large, copper-colored Chagoi. More than two and a half feet long, this fish had been a favorite with the toddler breakfast crowd. I inspected it quickly and noted the beginnings of fin rot, an external symptom of liver damage. Fish and pastries don't mix, folks.

I looked at the fish. I looked at my bucket. "We're gonna need a bigger bucket," I muttered.

There was no one to laugh (not that anyone would have) and the clock was ticking, so I put the garbage bag over my hands like a giant glove, grabbed the floating fish corpse, and inverted the bag. Working fast, I knotted the top and dumped the whole thing into the bucket, where it landed with a thunk and a squelch. The bucket tottered for a second and flipped, landing with an echoing clatter and flinging the bag o'fish onto the pavers with a loud splat. I retrieved the fish and tried a few different orientations, but it slipped and slid and generally resisted my efforts to stuff it securely in the bucket.

By this point the lunch crowd was making distressed noises so I gave up on the bucket and hoisted the whole mess into my arms, hugging it to my chest while the tail flopped freely. I pulled out my phone, texted "got it" to my mom and, noting the time, discarded the idea of popping into Josephine's for a cookie and a latte. Maybe my luck would turn and I'd have a second to hit the vending machines at school before my next class.

I trudged out of La Arcada as quickly as I could given the twenty pounds of dead carp in my arms, hauling my load past the library and into the city garage where I'd parked the truck. I tossed the koi into my truck bed and gave my arms an exploratory sniff. Not too fishy!

I drove to the exit, fed my ticket into the payment machine, and pulled slowly through the toll gate, careful to keep Shelob clear of the kiosk. This was good. I had twelve minutes until AP Physics. If my parking spot was still empty I'd be able to run by the vending island and grab a Kit Kat before the late bell.

As I neared Anacapa Street, a black BMW pulled the wrong way into the exit driveway, approaching me head-on. I hit the brakes and braced. Seconds from impact, the car swerved sideways and pulled off onto a narrow maintenance strip painted with diagonal stripes and the words "No Parking." I stared in disbelief as the driver's door opened.

He emerged from the car all damp hair, board shorts, and Ray-Bans, his tanned chest on full display. Glancing my way, he grinned in recognition. "Gotta get some rezzies!" he called, then jogged *away from the car* and through the doorway of a nearby sushi restaurant, shrugging into a shirt as he went.

I turned back to the BMW, which sat mostly out of the way on the striped shoulder. Directly across from it, on the raised concrete median, stood a yellow "Watch For Pedestrians" sign on a metal pole. Squeezing between the two would be tight but doable . . . unless you happened to have a large, fiberglass spider bolted to the side of your vehicle.

I hit the horn. Waited. Honked again. The door to the sushi restaurant remained closed.

At this rate, there wasn't going to be any bad luck left for the rest of the world. I was hogging all of it. Honestly, what were the odds? I was going to be late to school twice in the same day. Thanks to Spencer Salazar. Spencer-freaking-Salazar. Grade-A entitled trustifarian slacker—and my next door neighbor. On both sides. Also my backyard neighbor. Basically, I'm surrounded by Spencer Salazar. My house occupies one of the tiny parcels of land along the street that the fifties-era developers of our seaside neighborhood carved out of the deep, oceanfront lots. Spencer's dad purchased the houses on both sides of mine and demolished them, building a garage to the left and a swimming pool and cabana to the right. (My dad declined to sell, so the Salazars' pétanque court remains an unrealized dream.) Behind all of this, their house stretches along 150 feet of cliff-top ocean frontage, offering the Salazars an unobstructed view of the Pacific and the Channel Islands beyond. I, on the other hand, have an unobstructed view of the six-foot wall that separates my yard from Spencer's.

Well, Spencer's dad is a famous author. My dad is a bug man.

I didn't resent Spencer because of his amazing house or his father's fame. This was Santa Barbara, after all, a town where every parking lot looked like a Range Rover rally and even English royalty got busted for using the jogging track without a membership. No, I couldn't stand Spencer Salazar because he was the most worthless person on the planet. Really. He literally slept through freshman English class. Some days he even snored. He threw loud pool parties that kept me up at night (after which his friends sometimes vomited in my yard). He threw Funyuns over the wall to my dog (after which my dog sometimes vomited in my yard). And now he had imprisoned me in a toll lane with a mere ten minutes remaining until the start of my next class.

Spencer Salazar was a scourge.

Thanks to the scourge, I starved all through AP Physics, then, at the bell, burned precious minutes in line for the physics presentation sign-up sheet. I could have signed up later and hit the snack machines but all the good topics had already been snapped up before class. If I delayed any longer, I risked ending up with Capacitance and Dielectrics or something. When I at last reached the front, I scrawled my name by Torque and jogged off, still hungry, to Virtual Enterprise.

Montana waved at me from a desk by the windows and motioned me over. I slid into an empty seat and she pushed a paper bag toward me.

"Here," she said. "Yogurt parfait."

Not my favorite—I'd eaten a lot of yogurt in the year following my parents' divorce, until Rachael Ray taught me how to use the stove—but the temporary mood-bump I'd gotten from depositing the dead carp in Spencer Salazar's trunk had long since faded. I needed some sugar. "Thanks," I said, extracting a spoon and a plastic container from the bag.

"So," she asked, "how'd the fish rescue go?"

"It wasn't exactly a rescue . . ." I froze as Spencer Salazar appeared in the doorway. Speak of the devil. Okay, maybe the dead fish thing had been a tad extreme. But, seriously, Life Lesson Number One: Don't block traffic like a jackass. Life Lesson Number Two? If you're going to block traffic like a jackass, lock your car.

"What's Spencer Salazar doing in here?" I hissed. I slapped the lid back on my parfait, preparing to bolt.

Montana gave me a funny look. "He's in this class. Remember? He took all the prereqs with us last spring."

"Oh." I did not remember but I relaxed a little—still keeping a wary eye on Spencer—until a strange noise coming from Montana caught my attention.

"Are you growling?" I asked.

"It's *her*. How could they let her in this class? You have to take Marketing and Computer Business first."

Britta Verhaag stood in the doorway surveying the scene. Her neutral expression turned sour as she spotted Spencer. Well, we had that in common. I wondered if he made a habit of blocking traffic.

I turned to Montana. "You know, when we saw her this morning, you failed to mention her last name was Verhaag."

Montana was still glaring at Britta. "So?"

"So . . . guess who's now eligible for the Verhaag Scholarship this year? You know, *my* Verhaag Scholarship?"

Montana's gaze shot to mine, her mouth forming a horrified *O*. "Oh, god, do you think she'll submit a paper?"

I held up my hands. *Of course.*

"Do you want me to rejoin the team? Ugh, that wouldn't even work. She's not giving up that captain spot. Hal, I'm sorry." She tapped her pen on the desk and looked like she was thinking hard. Finally she shook her head. "You're so screwed."

I dropped my head onto my desk.

"Afternoon, everyone." The teacher walked in.

"I am *so* sorry!" Montana whispered.

Me too, I mouthed silently.

My last class of the day was Italian Cinema. We were watching *The Bicycle Thief,* which paired nicely with the dismal demise of all my dreams. I could totally relate to Antonio. The Verhaag Scholarship was my bicycle and, without it, my dream was *senza speranza.* In one sense, Antonio actually had it better than me. I mean, we weren't sleeping on bare mattresses at my house, but at least he had options. I walked out to my truck pondering how many bicycles I'd have to steal in order to pay for a semester at Georgetown.

"Hey!" A short guy wearing an *Atlas Shrugged* t-shirt stood by the grey Tesla, his fists braced on his hips. "You need to find somewhere else to park. You're all over my parking space."

"My bad," I told him. "Which of these spaces is yours?" I indicated the two spaces he'd parked diagonally across. On-campus parking spots were in such demand, anyone arriving extra-late usually had to park on the street. It took a special kind of snowflake to park in two of them.

He glared at me. "You blocked me yesterday, too. I can't get my door open with your stupid spider in the way."

Oh no. He did not just insult Shelob.

I gave him a blank look. "Spider? Where?"

"The giant spider on your truck."

I gave my head a small shake.

He pointed. "Right there. Giant freaking spider! Are you on the spectrum or something?"

Wasn't he a peach? I held his gaze and slid slowly behind the wheel. "Giant spiders. Ohhh-kay. I'm gonna go now." I slammed the door and started the truck, then carefully pulled forward out of the spot. As I turned toward the exit, he appeared in my passenger-side window shaking his finger and yelling, "Don't park by me anymore!"

I gave him a thumbs up and drove off. I was totally parking next to him tomorrow.

As soon as I was clear of campus, I pulled into an empty driveway to put on my work shirt and check for schedule updates. Consulting the jobs app on my phone, I realized the routine ant treatment in San Roque I'd been assigned that morning had been replaced. Puzzled, I pulled up the address on the new work ticket then dialed Autumn, our office manager.

"Hey, what happened to my ant spray?" I asked.

"I gave it to Chuy. They want you in Montecito."

"I went out there this morning."

"They want you back."

"Did they schedule a fumigation?"

"No, they just want you back out."

"Did they say why?"

"Nope." *Click.*

Autumn isn't what you'd call a people person.

Fifteen minutes later I was asking Irma the same question. Politely, of course.

"Fumigation sounds serious. How many people come out for that? Just you?"

"For the fumigation?" I eyed the roof of the guest cottage. "It takes a whole crew to get the tent on. About four guys. I'm usually in school when they do them."

"Well," she said dismissively, "my boss says no poison in the air. He wants something natural."

Ugh, California. You know what's natural? Rats.

"There's really no danger," I assured her. "The tent contains all the fumigant and it dissipates very quickly once the tent comes down."

We also add a strong tear gas as a warning agent. You'd notice the tear gas way before you breathed in toxic levels of anything, but I didn't mention this. People hear "tear gas" and, for some reason, they freak right out.

Irma was already shaking her head. "My boss says for you just to use traps."

Okay, I hate traps. I don't do squirrel calls and I rarely take gopher jobs. Everyone in the office knows this and mostly respects my limits because, after all, I didn't exactly choose this career path. Autumn had only sent me on this job because it was supposed to be an estimate, followed by a visit from our fumigation team. Rats are several significant rungs down the cute-and-fuzzy ladder from squirrels, but they're still mammals, and I was not feeling very happy at that moment.

Still, if I didn't do something, I couldn't charge for the visit. I considered my options. There were, in my estimation, a buttload of rats in that attic. The Haffkine Institute in Mumbai, India, makes a trap that can catch up to twenty-five rats at once. Supercool—if rat-catching is your thing—but my dad won't spring for one. At his insistence, I carry snap traps. Snap traps are exactly what they sound like, and they catch one rat apiece. I had three snap traps in the truck, which wouldn't make a dent in this rat population, and rats, being pretty smart, wouldn't take the bait from these anyway.

So there was that, at least.

"Okay," I agreed.

Irma led me inside the guest cottage, which was essentially one large room with a sleeping area on one side and a living area on the other. On the far side of an enormous bed, the only interior door stood wide open, revealing a bathroom with a large shower. Evidence of the capital letter Guests was everywhere, with clothes, shoes, and even jewelry and cash strewn on every flat surface. I was glad to have Irma with me. Montecito had been experiencing a recent wave of thefts and break-ins and residents were on edge. This added an extra layer of thrill to my job because now half the estate owners had their people-eating Rhodesian ridgebacks patrolling the property in broad daylight and they didn't always remember to kennel Scooter and Franz when their friendly pest control technician was scheduled to visit. Even under normal circumstances, this was exactly the kind of situation where something could turn up missing and the first response would be to blame the bug girl. Much easier than accusing the house staff, which could make your stay unpleasant, or just admitting you were pathologically messy and had probably left your Hermès watch out by the hot tub.

Irma pointed out the hatch over the living area from which the attic stairs pulled down. There was no cord, just a shiny silver ring pull.

"How do I reach the pull?" I asked.

She fetched a polished wooden pole with a shiny silver hook at the end from an umbrella stand by the door and handed it over. I looked at the pole, which was maybe three feet long, then at the hatch, which was probably ten feet from the ground, then at Irma, who shrugged.

After opening the hatch—a maneuver that required me to balance precariously on the back of the sofa while waving a pointy hook around—I climbed most of the way up the telescoping attic stairs—which flexed concerningly beneath the soles of my Vans—and shoved the traps just inside the opening. Since I was charging for the visit, I did it properly, leaving the traps un-set and un-baited. I would come back in a week, after the rats had marked them as safe (i.e., peed on them) to set and bait them. Well, ideally, I'd be back in a week to collect my traps after the fumigation guys had done their thing. I handed Irma an invoice and headed off to my next call.

To which I was going to be very late. A loose goat on the 101 had caused a three-car pileup and traffic was at a standstill.

The US-101 is the only major artery on this entire stretch of coast. People here are always gushing about how nice it is to live in a place that isn't paved over with interstates, and tourists seem to love the 101 for its scenic views of the ocean on one side and the wildflower-covered mountains on the other. If you want my opinion, scenic is overrated. Out-of-lane collisions caused by drivers checking the surf as they pass Rincon Point is the number four cause of traffic delays in this region. It takes almost nothing to close down the 101 and, as the KCLU News Team can attest, inconvenient things happen on the 101 on a near-daily basis: baby cribs blocking the two left lanes, a truckload of anchovies spilled on the southbound, last week there was a guy on an electric unicycle weaving through traffic . . . a live goat was par for the course.

At any rate, I wasn't going anywhere this decade, so when my phone rang, I answered it. It was, of course, my mother. I rested my forehead on the steering wheel, "Mom. I'm having a really bad day—"

"*Eeeee*, Hallie, we have the best news!"

"We" in my mom's case usually includes her husband, Grant. Grant is an immigration attorney and reasonably cool guy. He's very calm, which makes him a refreshing contrast to my mom, and very dedicated to his job. He takes on a lot of pro bono asylum cases, so he doesn't make much money, but he saves lives. My dad refers to him exclusively as "that liberal idiot."

"Oh? Okay. Hi, Grant."

"Hello, Hal. What's—"

My mom jumped in. "We're having a baby!"

My jaw dropped so hard the joint cracked.

"Isn't that amazing? Can you believe it? After all this time! Oh, and it'll be born in March—a Pisces! I'm so excited to have a Pisces. No offense, sweetheart, but you Capricorns are so independent."

I closed my mouth and managed a faint "Wow."

"I know! You're coming to dinner tonight, right? We can talk all about it. I'm pretty sure we conceived—"

Grant, thank god, cut in at that moment. "How are things with you, Hal? You mentioned a bad day?"

To my horror, my eyes flooded with tears. I blinked hard and took a deep breath, held it, let it out slowly. "I lost my chance at the Verhaag Scholarship," I told them. My voice sounded almost normal.

For a moment there was nothing but silence. Then my mom exclaimed, "You'll be staying here for college—you'll be able to babysit!"

"Heidi," I heard Grant say softly.

"What?" my mom said. "You wait until you see what decent babysitters charge."

"I'm sorry, Hal," Grant offered. "I know how hard you've been working on that."

"Who says you lost your chance?" my mom demanded. Conversations with my mom have been known to cause whiplash. "Your paper will be the best paper they've ever read."

My mom had never read my paper but she genuinely believes everything I do is the best ever. She's logical like that.

"Britta Verhaag just transferred to Santa Barbara High."

"Oh," Grant said heavily.

"Who's Britta Verhaag?" my mom asked. "I bet her paper won't be half as good as yours."

I tapped my forehead against the steering wheel. "Mom. It's the *Verhaag* Scholarship."

"So?"

"They always give it to Verhaag kids if there's any graduating from the school that year," Grant explained, like it wasn't at all odd for her to be ignorant of the finer details of an endeavor I'd been wholly focused on for *three years*.

"Always," I agreed glumly.

"What?" my mom sounded outraged. "That's ridiculous. This is America."

Grant was assuring her that nepotism was a traditionally American value, when a goat appeared by my door. The goat shied at the sight of the giant spider looming over him and, with an alarmed bleat, jumped over the concrete barrier that separated my lane from traffic heading the opposite direction. Seconds later, I heard brakes screeching and the sharp crunch of colliding metal. Uh-oh.

My mom said my name, dragging my attention away from my

sideview mirror. "Well, Hallie, if the Verhaags really do things that way, I don't know why you wasted all your time on this scholarship."

Wow. Thanks, Mom. "How was I supposed to know a Verhaag would transfer into my class at the last minute?"

"At the last minute!" my mom exclaimed. "Sweetie, I know you like to think I'm the space cadet in this family, but your ability to tune out the people around you, it's . . . well . . . you get it from your father."

"Um," Grant said.

"Mom, what are you even talking about?"

"Hallie," she said with exaggerated patience, "there's been a Verhaag in your class since ninth grade."

Bull. "No. There hasn't."

"Uh, yes, there has."

"Who?" I demanded.

"Honestly, Hallie, you've known him your whole life, how could you possibly—"

"*Who?*"

"DON'T YELL AT ME, I'M PREGNANT!"

"Ladies," Grant said appeasingly.

"Oh, quiet, Grant," my mom said. "We're fine. Hallie, it's Spencer. Spencer Salazar."

CHAPTER 3

So there it was. The Plan hadn't been ruined in the eleventh hour by dance team politics; The Plan had been doomed from the start. There had been a Verhaag there all along and, of course, *of course*, it was Spencer-freaking-Salazar. The knowledge pounded around in my head like sneakers in a clothes dryer: Spencer Salazer was a Verhaag. He didn't live in Montecito, or play polo, and his last name wasn't even Verhaag—although, according to my mom, his mother's was. Or had been until she'd married Oscar Salazar. Spencer was like one of those terrorist cells—a sleeper Verhaag. I could blame my lack of due diligence or my mother's peripatetic interest in my hopes and dreams, but it hardly mattered. The outcome was the hot, steaming knowledge that I squandered three years analyzing crap poetry ("The Cremation of Sam McGee": seriously, why?) and researching the life and times of a college drop-out (I mean, really. Who drops out of McGill? I would kill to go to McGill!) raccoon coat–wearing wannabe who'd moved to Alaska and stayed drunk and probably very stinky until he finally made all the money off said crap poetry and moved to Paris. A place that *I* would never move, or probably even visit, because I was going to be stuck in Santa Barbara *forever*.

All that work. All of it for nothing.

My next two service calls were routine—a good thing, as I wasn't feeling very focused—and I was back at the shop a little after five to drop off my empty tanks.

"Hal, come in here!" I heard my dad call from inside the garage.

Still distracted, I missed Autumn's urgent head-shake and walked right in. I caught my first glimpse and tried to back right out again but it was too late.

"Come on over, pickle," my dad ordered. "I need you to Facebook these for me."

Three stiff, dead gophers lay belly-up on the lid of my dad's aluminum truck box, mouths agape, claws fully extended. My dad is the kind of devoted small-business owner who embraces all marketing opportunities and, last Christmas, my aunt gave him a copy of *Social Media Marketing for Dummies*. He'd been ponderously working his way through it, taking notes as he went, for the past nine months.

"I'd do it myself but I forgot my damn password again." He reached out and adjusted the angle of the middle gopher so it lay perfectly parallel to its unfortunate buddies. "Here, get a photo. I have a great 'before' pic I'll text you. And don't forget to mention that we have nerve gas."

Through the open office door, I spied Autumn at her desk giving me the evil eye. In addition to being his office manager, Autumn is my dad's long-term girlfriend and she is very invested in both roles. She keeps our appointments tight, our customers happy, and she makes sure my dad doesn't find out about Instagram.

"Any luck resetting that password?" my dad called to her.

"Working on it, Pete," she replied.

I held up both hands in a helpless gesture and she rolled

her eyes at me. I obediently snapped a photo of the gophers and posted it to the Mayhew Pest Control page while my dad observed over my shoulder. I hoped it wouldn't get too many views before I got a chance to delete it.

"Great," my dad gave my shoulder a satisfied pat. "That'll grab 'em. Make sure you Twitter it too." He walked around to the other side of the truck and started unloading his tanks. "How was school?"

I met his eyes across a landscape of dead gophers. "I lost the Verhaag Scholarship."

"What? I thought they didn't award that for weeks."

"Three weeks," I corrected. "But Britta Verhaag transferred into my class today from DP. And, according to—" My brain stopped my mouth just in time. Any mention of my mom would bring the useful portion of this conversation to an abrupt end. I gave my head a regretful shake. "Well. It's over."

My dad continued unloading his tanks then moved on to gopher disposal. When all that was done he said, "Well, maybe you can get a different scholarship."

I didn't bother responding.

"Look, pickle," he came around the truck and slung his arm over my shoulders, "I've told you before: you don't need a fancy East Coast college to succeed in life. You can go to the City College for free. That's an amazing opportunity. And, if you want to transfer after two years, UC Santa Barbara is a great school. I hear their entomology department is doing big things. It'll be perfect for you. You can keep working with me while you get your degree." He nudged me with his hip. "We have a good time, right? And, someday, all this will be yours."

I stared at him in horror. If he thought I wanted to study

bugs *or* run a pest control company, he needed to be more careful around the termite fumigant.

"What? Look, we'll talk about it at dinner, okay? We're going over to Autumn's. She's making chilaquiles."

"Can't," I reminded him. "I'm having dinner at Mom's."

His face took on this sort of pinched expression he got whenever my mom was mentioned. I knew he thought it looked "neutral," which was the favorite word of the family therapist we saw right after the divorce. It did not look neutral.

"Okay, good. Tomorrow then," he said, not quite sounding neutral, either.

I realized this was probably the moment to mention my mom's pregnancy but, seriously, I didn't get paid enough to deal with this stuff.

"I'll be home by eight," I said, as I always did, and headed for the parking lot.

"You tell me if that liberal idiot smokes anything while you're there," he yelled after me. "Love you!"

I got into my truck, put my hands on the wheel, and just sat there, thinking. My mom was expecting me. Yup, she was cooking up some kind of vegan awfulness infused with an extra helping of overbearing love, right now, all for me. We would talk about the baby, and whatever she thought I should do next year now that my college plans were ruined. So great.

I made no move to start the car.

I thought of my dad inside the shop, getting ready to head to Autumn's for dinner. I imagined Autumn scowling at me over soggy nachos.

Then I pictured my house. My empty house. Nobody home but the dog.

My mom would be so disappointed if I bailed on dinner, especially tonight. Then again, the dog would be awfully lonely if I didn't. He'd been by himself all afternoon, and who knew what time my dad would be home?

I picked up my phone and sent my mom a quick text: Tons of homework. Gotta skip dinner. Tomorrow instead?

My phone rang immediately but I couldn't answer. I was already on the road.

At six p.m. on an August Wednesday, the sun had just begun to soften in the Santa Barbara sky. A gentle breeze off the Pacific ruffled palm fronds and bougainvillea as it swept across the Mesa, and the bike lane in front of my house was blocked off with orange cones for Nite Moves, the weekly 5k, though none of the runners had made it up the hill yet. At seven o'clock I would be out in my front yard getting the mail because, at seven o'clock, on the dot, one of the guys doing the aquathlon would run by in his Speedo. If I was home, I never missed Speedo guy but, with an hour to spare, I continued on through the front door and allowed myself to be pounced on by our dog, Roundup.

Roundup is a one hundred and twenty pound akita, so allowing him to pounce takes commitment. Akitas are basically giant cats, though, so the pouncing never lasts long. That would be undignified. I hooked a leash to his collar and walked him to the end of the block and around the corner to our beach access, known around here as Thousand Steps. There aren't quite a thousand steps in the slippery concrete staircase but there are enough to make the trip back up exciting if you're carrying boogie boards or beach chairs. Tonight it was just me, the dog, and a roll of poo bags. I unclipped Roundup's leash at the bottom of the steps and he sprinted off in search of tide pool treasure. I stretched out on a flat boulder, still hot from the sun, and moped while he chewed on seaweed and romped with some passing labradors. When I got hungry, we hiked back up the stairs, Roundup moving considerably more slowly than he had on the way down, and trudged home.

I made a cheese sandwich in the toaster oven, grabbed a juice out of the fridge, and followed Roundup into the backyard. There I flopped onto the grass and went to work on my sandwich, absently shoving Roundup's head away when he tried to steal a bite.

It all just sucked. So bad. For three years I had seriously worked my butt off, saving every penny I made from working two jobs, taking a full advanced course load, doing endless test prep, and, of course, sinking. Every. Spare. Second. Into crafting the world's most artful and well-researched load of bull about the English language's worst poet. I hadn't gone to a single party. I had barely seen my friends. I couldn't even remember what the inside of a movie theater looked like. Three years of drudgery I could never take back. And the five years to come? Those were looking even worse. Those were—

Thup.

Something small and extremely lightweight bounced off my forehead and landed in the grass. Roundup pounced and gulped it down before I could identify it.

Thup.

This one hit my arm. I formed an impression of something white and fluffy before Roundup ate that one too. The third made no noise at all, as Roundup snatched that one out of the air.

I sprang to my feet and marched to the wall bordering the right side of my backyard. Scrambling onto the lid of the fiberglass dock box my dad kept there for storing gardening stuff, I grabbed the top of the wall and hoisted myself upward until I could hook my armpits over the top.

On the other side of the wall, Spencer Salazar lounged on a cushioned teak pool chaise with a Costco-sized bag of Pirate's Booty in his lap. As I watched, he stuffed a white cheddar puff into his mouth then idly threw another over his shoulder. It flew past my head and was fielded below by Roundup.

"Hey!" I barked.

Spencer jerked in surprise and craned his head back until he spotted me, perched on his wall like an angry crow. "Oh, hey."

"Stop feeding my dog."

"He likes it."

"It's bad for him. Keep that crap to yourself."

Spencer glanced down at the bag in his lap then slid off the chaise and headed for the wall. Two broad hands appeared on the top, next to my arms.

"What are you—ack!" The rest of Spencer appeared beside his hands and I let go in surprise, landing with a loud *thud* on the dock box. Spencer pivoted, shifting his legs across to my side of the wall, and followed me down.

Roundup shot to his feet and did his impression of a curly-tailed gargoyle of doom. Akitas don't bark much but when they do, they mean it. The bag of Pirate's Booty reappeared from wherever Spencer had stashed it—the waistband of his board shorts, maybe?—and Roundup fell abruptly silent.

Spencer held the bag out. "You should try it. It's tasty. And it's made of rice. Rice is good for you, right?"

"Not really."

"Huh." Spencer turned his attention to my yard, looking around curiously. There wasn't much to see. A small patio of brick pavers with a table, four chairs, and a stainless steel grill; a neat row of iceberg rosebushes planted a careful three feet from the foundation of the house; and the open slider, through which our kitchen with its tiled counters and circa 1950s cabinets was clearly visible. To the right of that, a second, smaller slider led to my room, giving Spencer a nice view of several towering piles of folded laundry atop my full-sized bed. The contrast between my backyard and the *Architectural Digest*-worthy tableau just over the wall was striking.

"Nice grass," Spencer commented.

Well, it was: freshly trimmed, lush, and emerald green. Drought, schmout, as far as my dad was concerned.

It occurred to me that Spencer seemed pretty chill for a guy who had recently discovered a dead fish in the trunk of his German luxury car. It wouldn't take much detecting to figure out who put it there, although, to be honest, Spencer didn't seem like much of a detective.

"Sorry about blocking you in earlier," he offered. "Big family dinner tonight and I told my mom I'd make the reservations last week."

I couldn't help scowling at the mention of Spencer's scholarship-hogging, dream-killing family.

"Did I make you late for class?"

I gritted my teeth. "Only slightly."

"Oh, okay. 'Cause just now you looked really mad."

I looked up and met Spencer's surprisingly steady gaze. I realized that this was the closest I'd been to Spencer in years. We lived mere feet from each other but I rarely saw him outside of school. His light, gray eyes were kind of striking set against his brown skin and black hair.

"Well," I blurted out, "you did steal my scholarship."

Spencer's dark eyebrows went up. "I what?"

I blinked hard, hoping to reset my brain. "Eh. Forget I said that."

"No-o-o," Spencer said consideringly, "I don't think I can do that. Explain, please."

My shoulders slumped. It had been a long day. A long, bad day. All I wanted to do was lie down in my yard and brood for a few more minutes—oh, and ogle Speedo guy—before plunging into my nightly sinkhole of homework. And neither of those things would happen if I couldn't get Spencer back on his side of the wall. "Look," I offered. "I didn't mean that how it sounded. It's actually your cousin who's stealing my scholarship—although I guess you could be stealing it too—but now I'll never get out of this town and I'll have to spend the next five years killing vermin and changing diapers and it's all just really freaking depressing."

Spencer stared at me. "That's the most I've heard you say in years, and none of it made any sense."

I tried to remember if Spencer had been this aggravating as a little kid. Probably.

"Do you think you could clarify some of that?" he persisted.

I checked the time on my phone. So much for brooding. "I gotta get the mail."

"This second?"

I turned and walked into the house, abandoning Spencer in my backyard. I mean, whatever. He knew the way home. The clock on the stove read 6:57. I quickened my step, hustling through the kitchen and living room, out the front door, and down the driveway.

A strong tide of runners now flowed up the street. Across the way, Montana and Madison were stationed at the end of their driveway, their petite butts parked in a couple of beach chairs. They each held a set of pompoms, which they shook encouragingly when anyone they knew ran by. They waved at me and I waved back.

"Just in time! Almost seven!" Madison shouted.

"What happens at seven?" a deep voice asked from behind me.

I jumped at least a foot and turned to glare at Spencer. "Did you walk through my house?"

"Yes."

"Go home."

"You were explaining."

"No, I wasn't."

Montana and Madison shook their pompoms at me, grabbing my attention. Madison pointed at Spencer and widened her eyes questioningly. I shrugged.

Spencer glanced across the street. "What are all of you doing out here?"

The alarm tone on Madison's phone went off. Montana, Madison, and I turned as one to look up the street. Around the corner came Speedo guy, his swimmer/runner's body glistening with sea water and sweat. The three of us watched appreciatively as he ran by at a quick, steady pace and disappeared into the distance. Montana and Madison stood, folded their beach chairs, and gave me another wave before disappearing into their garage.

I grabbed the day's mail from my mailbox and glanced at Spencer, who was watching me with a funny look on his face. He opened his mouth to say something then seemed to change his mind. He pressed his lips together and gave his head a slow shake. I ignored him and walked back up the driveway and into my house. And this time I locked the door behind me.

CHAPTER 4

D r. McLoren's door was wide open when I arrived at his office the next morning. His visitor's chair, however, was already occupied, and in it sat none other than Britta Verhaag.

"Am I supposed to read all those?" she was asking Dr. McLoren as he handed her a thick packet of papers.

"Only if you'd like to know what to write about," he informed her dryly.

"Like it even matters. Isn't the deadline, like, tomorrow? Anything I write is going to be a load of crap. As if I could even type something that long in time." Scowling, she flipped through the packet. "Honestly, I have enough on my plate right now. Those hippos from the Sorcerer Mickey movie could put on a better routine than this so-called dance team. And I'm supposed to have them presentable by Homecoming? I do not have time for this."

I gripped the doorframe as, deep in my soul, a spark of hope reignited.

"You'll find the deadline right there on the cover page," Dr. McLoren indicated on his own packet. "You have several days to work on your submission, should you feel inclined to enter."

"If I'd known my parents were going to hassle me about this I'd have stayed at DP." Britta slapped the packet closed in annoyance. "My dad is all, 'Verhaags always win the Verhaag

Scholarship. It's your legacy.' And Spencer's not even entering, that bum." She paused. "I mean, even if Spencer *were* entering, I would totally win it. Just because his dad's an author, he thinks he's special. We're *both* descended from Richard W. Service, thank you very much."

"Robert," Dr. McLoren corrected.

"Hmm? Anyway, my dad says if I write this stupid essay he'll get me a condo in Malibu when I go to Pepperdine next year. And, when I win, I'll be in the paper. God knows that won't be happening because of dance team. Mimes have better moves." She gave a small huff of disgust. "Okay, fine. I'll do it."

Hope died.

"Wonderful," Dr. McLoren commented, his face void of expression.

Britta hopped up and left without a word, brushing past me in the doorway, her stride somehow perfectly balanced on platform Miu Miu espadrilles.

I stuck my head through the door and Dr. McLoren motioned me in. "Good morning, Hal. Sorry you had to see that."

Not half as sorry as I was. "So it's definitely happening?"

He lifted his hands in a helpless gesture. "Her submission requires my approval, but as long as it conforms with the guidelines, I must accept it."

Pretty much what I'd expected. A thought occurred to me. "Did you know Spencer Salazar is a Verhaag?"

Dr. McLoren looked chagrinned. "I discovered that little tidbit last spring. But I met with Mr. Salazar at that time and he assured me he does not plan to pursue the scholarship because he won't be applying to a bachelor's program. I would have mentioned it but I didn't believe he would affect your chances in any way."

So Spencer wasn't even going to college. Why didn't that surprise me? Actually, it did surprise me. There were tiny private colleges all over the country, schools with strong Greek systems and guaranteed entry for rich kids who could afford sixty grand a year to party with other rich kids. I would have expected Spencer to go that route, maybe after a gap year surfing in Indonesia or something.

"But I'm afraid Miss Verhaag intends to win by wickets, as they say on the cricket field, so—" He handed me several pages of printouts and folded his hands on his desktop—"let's talk extracurriculars."

There was no hope for it. Without the Verhaag scholarship, I had just one path forward: pad my college application with enough irrelevant BS to qualify for the free City College bequest. If I really applied myself, I might be able to transfer to UCSB after two years and cap off my education with some in-depth study of Functional Insect Morphology. All while living with my dad. Oh, my stars were looking very bright, indeed.

I idly wondered how much Britta would pay me for my essay before dismally recalling she could submit twenty-five pages of *lorem ipsum* dummy text and still win the damn thing. I turned my attention to the printouts.

Five minutes later we were still in the Bs.

"Backgammon club?"

Did ninety-year-olds go to high school now? "No."

"Bird-watchers club?"

The only birds I had experience watching were the ones I sometimes pulled out of attics. Those were always dead. "No."

"Bridle club?"

"What is that, horses? Too rich for my blood." I dropped my

list and rubbed my forehead. "I mean, what would look good on a transcript that won't take much time or cost any money?"

"Well . . ." Dr. McLoren fiddled with a pen and stared at the ceiling. "I hear yearbook staff needs people."

Thus, after Italian Cinema, I tracked down Leah Steiger. Leah and I had partnered on a few group projects back in tenth grade biology and, thanks to her mad scrapbooking skills, we'd killed it with our visual aids. You haven't seen a diagram of earthworm anatomy until you've seen one with a layered leaf collage and shadow-boxed excretory organs.

For my part, I'd written an A+ earthworm paper, earning us both an exemption from the midterm exam, so I was surprised when she greeted my request with a dark scowl.

"I figured I could write copy or something," I explained.

"Well, *I* would love to have you on staff but *I* am not in charge this year."

"Huh?" Leah had been assistant yearbook editor last year and the yearbook hierarchy was iron-clad. This was Leah's year to shine, or crop, or whatever the Grand Pooh-Bah of yearbook staff does.

Leah looked like she was about to angry-cry. I tried not to smile. Wearing that expression, she was a total doppelgänger for the little Sadness character from *Inside Out*. Blue hair and all. It was uncanny.

"There was an incident with the yearbook supplements in July."

"The yearbook whats?" I was not a yearbook purchaser. I did not have ninety dollars to spend on photos of people I could look at for free any time I wanted.

She gave me an impatient look. "Supplements. Extra pages

that cover stuff that happens after we send the volume to print. They glue into the backs of the yearbooks. Except last year's disappeared out of the yearbook room before we could distribute them. And, since Seraphina had already graduated, Mrs. Ritter held me responsible. Tyler Lofaro's dad paid for a whole new set of supplements to be printed up and so guess who she replaced me with."

Wow, first the dance team upset and now this. I had no idea extracurricular leadership roles were so fraught with drama.

"That sucks." I paused for a moment to convey sympathy. "So, I should talk to Tyler?"

Leah glared. Oops. I made a note to pause longer next time. "Yeah," she said. "Do that."

The yearbook room was a large, windowless cave located at the end of a maintenance hallway across from the student council lounge. The newspaper staff had a choice location in Building A, with skylights and one of those expensive coffee machines built into the wall, but yearbook was not so prestigious an enterprise. As I approached, I noticed that the student council lounge at least got windows—though, even with the ventilation, the combined odors of Sharpies and rabid ambition wafting from that room permeated the hallway.

The door to the yearbook room was open, and inside, a woman with wild, apricot-colored hair was fiddling with a media cart and speaking to a group of freshman. "This video will show you how to use InDesign to create a yearbook layout. I want the three of you . . . what in the world?" She looked up and called to the room at large, "Why is there a quesadilla in the DVD player?"

Maybe this wasn't such a great idea. I could learn to love birds. They weren't so bad when they weren't decomposing.

I started to back away and bumped into Leah, who gave me a

42

surprised look. "Hey, you're serious?" she asked. "You really want to join yearbook?"

"Umm . . ."

"Who wants to join yearbook?" The orange-haired woman spun around and beamed at me in delight. "Come right in!"

Leah towed me through the door and I cast a wary look around the space. This soon after the bell, the room was sparsely populated. A kid in a Hawaiian shirt sat with his feet propped on a desk and his face hidden behind a book titled *Fanfiction 101.* Two juniors stood by a cabinet arguing over a digital camera, and one of the freshmen by the media cart was now eating a moldy-looking quesadilla.

And in the back, jumping up from behind a Mac station, was Tesla Boy.

"No," he said, predictably. "She is not joining yearbook staff."

Leah ignored him. "Mrs. Ritter, Hallie is an excellent writer. I've worked with her before."

"Yeah," Tesla Boy rolled his eyes, "I'm sure she has an award-winning bedbug blog."

I shrugged. I had maybe written a post or two about bedbugs for my dad's blog.

"We don't let seniors just show up and be on staff," he continued. "You've got to pay your dues. She just wants the cred for her college application. It's not gonna happen."

Did he say *cred*?

Mrs. Ritter clucked disapprovingly. "Tyler, we welcome each and every student who feels called to journalism. Anyone with a passion for chronicling these precious years is an asset to our staff."

"*I'm* the editor," he said aggressively, "and the answer is no."

Mrs. Ritter gave me an apologetic look. "Why don't you come talk to me tomorrow during advisory period?"

"You're just the moderator. I've made the call. It's done," Tyler proclaimed. He gave me a look of disgust. "Now go move your crapbox truck—"

"Tyler!"

"—before I finish here. I'm not waiting on you again. I'll have you towed."

Well, okay then. I turned and left. I wasn't going to pitch a fit for the right to join yearbook staff. Obnoxious as he was, Tyler was right. I didn't give a crap about yearbooks—I'd never even bought one.

Leah chased me out the door. "Hal! I'm sorry about Tyler. If it were still up to me, I'd put you on staff right now."

"He's right," I told her. "My current interest is one hundred percent fueled by my college application needs."

She rolled her eyes. "Obviously."

I shrugged. "There are other clubs." If the birds didn't work out, I would learn backgammon.

She looked skeptical. "Other *serious* clubs that will enhance your applications without making you come to meetings after school? 'Cause I know you work in the afternoons."

I shrugged again. "Maybe?"

She grabbed my arm and dragged me further down the hall. "Listen. If you were on yearbook, we could assign you a couple of pages to work on and you could do them whenever you had time. In fact, if I were still in charge, I'd even give you an impressive title. 'Senior Section Editor' or something."

I couldn't work out her angle. "But you're not in charge. Parking Lot Napoleon is in charge."

She gave me a very intense look. "For now. You could help me with that."

"What?"

"I know Tyler stole those supplements so he could be editor," she said fiercely.

"Maybe," I agreed. From what I'd seen of Tyler, it seemed possible. Likely, even.

"Definitely," she corrected. "And if I can find them, I can prove he took them, and Mrs. Ritter will give me my job back."

"*If* he took them, don't you think he just threw them away?" That would be the smart thing to do.

"There were two thousand supplements in that order. Do you know how many boxes that is? That's a conspicuous amount to throw away, even in a full-sized dumpster. And I briefed all the city sanitation guys back in July."

Knowing Leah, she'd not only briefed all the city sanitation guys but checked their work. I wondered how much of her summer she'd spent dumpster diving.

She continued, "Trust me; if he tried to throw them away, I'd know about it."

"Okay, so?"

"So I know he's got them. I think they're at his house."

"Well, I doubt he's going to let you in to check."

"No," she gave me a significant look, "*I* can't go check. *I* have no reason to be walking around Tyler's house, or looking in Tyler's garage, or checking Tyler's attic. But, you know, I bet their friendly pest control technician could walk around his yard, no problem."

I waved my hands in front of me. "Oh, no. No, no, no. That is not how it works. I'm not the meter reader."

Leah continued, undaunted, "I bet they have a pest control

contract like everyone else in town and I've noticed the ants have been really bad lately . . ."

"Leah. That's illegal."

"You could just check and see if the Lofaros have a contract with your dad's company. If not, I'll drop it."

I was still shaking my head really fast.

"Just think about it," she pleaded. "You don't have to decide now. But yearbook would be perfect for you."

I'd already thought about it. There was no way. But I had a service appointment in ten minutes—yes, more ants—and I really had to go. "Okay, I'll think about it."

The very last thing I wanted to do after work that evening was drive all the way out to my mom's house, but there was no getting out of it two nights in a row. My mom and Grant have a small house up in the hills, down a winding, narrow road populated largely by artists and eccentrics. It's the kind of road where everyone crafts their own mailboxes from repurposed metal scraps or hand-carved tikis. Healing crystals and homemade wind chimes also feature prominently. Mom bought the house a couple of years after divorcing my dad and just before meeting Grant. It looks like it was built by a hobbit with a mosaic tile obsession and I am grateful every day of my life that I don't have to live there. I don't think it's exactly Grant's cup of tea, either, but it suits my mom perfectly.

Mom was considerably less chatty than usual—she mumbled something about morning sickness even though it was six p.m.— so, while she assembled the red bean and green grain taco bowls, I sat at her kitchen table paging through a list of registered extracurricular organizations. Sailing, salsa, squash . . . I wondered if those last two clubs were for enthusiasts of foods or activities. This list really should've come with descriptions.

We both looked up as Grant walked through the door with a briefcase and a giant smile on his face. "Hal," he announced with flourish, "I've found a solution to your Verhaag problem."

He explained as the two of us dug into our taco bowls (my mom had excused herself to go throw up), which weren't bad if you could get past the idea of wheat berries in a taco bowl. "I was giving the application guidelines a quick read and I found something interesting in the section on judging."

"I've read that part," I told him. "The final judging is conducted by the board members of the Verhaag Foundation, who are all Verhaags. And they always vote for Verhaags, if any apply."

"But did you read the footnote?" he asked, holding a page up at my eye level.

"There are footnotes? I never noticed any footnotes." I squinted across the table and, for the first time, noticed a tiny number at the end of one of the paragraphs.

"There is one footnote," Grant confirmed. "One very important footnote."

I grabbed the paper from him and studied it. There was no corresponding number above the bottom margin.

He pulled another page from the stack. "It's at the end. They added an extra page to the back rather than reformat the document." His expression was one of lawyerly disapproval. "Sloppy."

I reached for it just as he whipped it out of my grasp.

"Okay, so?!" I used my fork to crunch a tortilla chip into tiny pieces. "What does it say?"

"First, a little bit of background . . ."

I sighed.

"I called my friend Heather at the *News-Journal* and she tells me that, twenty-something years ago, Anastasia and Andrew Verhaag—twins—were both seniors at Santa Barbara High. Andrew, by the way, is Britta's father. Anyway, their aunt—one of the judges—tried to split the scholarship between the two, but there was no provision for that in the scholarship guidelines and her sister—their mother—objected. She wanted to award a full scholarship to each twin, but the Verhaag Foundation's charter prohibits them from issuing grants exceeding the amount of annual interest earned, and they'd already done a lot of giving that year. There wasn't enough money. Nobody in the family wanted to favor one twin over the other so someone came up with the idea to outsource the judging. They settled on the high school principal and the heads of two local organizations—probably friends of the family back then. Entirely different people now, of course. The Verhaags had their lawyers amend the guidelines to make it official, and no one ever bothered to take it out."

I could scarcely breathe. "So what does it say?"

He picked up the page and waived it in the air. "Should two or more members of the Verhaag family meet the eligibility requirements and apply for the Scholarship in a given year, judging shall be conducted by an alternate panel comprised of the Santa Barbara High School principal, the commodore of the Santa Barbara Yacht Club, and the president of the University Club of Santa Barbara."

I gave Grant a wide-eyed look. "So this means . . ."

He nodded. "This means you've got to get that kid next door to write a paper."

CHAPTER 5

The Shop is a small, counter-service restaurant run by a band of talented hipster-chefs and located a few blocks from my school. It shares space with a body shop and overlooks an uninspiring stretch of upper Milpas Street, but the speed of service and the tasty, eight-dollar burger box makes it a popular destination for SBHS students on lunch break. Montana, Madison, and I double-timed it to get there before all the shady tables were claimed. We pounced on the last one and I filled them in on the newest scholarship developments.

"That's awesome!" Madison exclaimed, clapping her hands in that elbow-out, flat-palmed way dancers and cheer-types always favor. "Your paper is amazing—oh my god, so much better than anything Britta can write!"

"With impartial judges, you'll definitely win," Montana agreed. "Grant's the jam."

I added ketchup to my black bean burger and said, "I'm not celebrating yet. We're talking about Spencer Salazar: Slacker Extraordinaire. He's not going to college. He barely even wears shirts. How am I supposed to convince him to write a research paper—assuming he even *can* write a research paper—for a scholarship he doesn't even want?"

"Spencer doesn't want to go to college?" Madison asked.

"I'm sure Spencer can write a research paper," Montana said firmly. "He's not an idiot. I know you guys don't hang out but you've heard him in class."

"Mmm," I said doubtfully. Virtual Enterprise was not that hard a class.

"You've got to ask him," Madison urged. "I *know* he'll do it. One time we were at the skate park watching, uhh, what's his name?"

"Anders." Montana sighed.

"Watching Anders show off for Monty—"

Who rolled her eyes.

"—and I got bored and wanted to go home but my bike tire was half deflated so Spencer let me take his bike and he rode mine home. All the way up the hill. With a practically flat tire." She raised a fist. "Bluff Drive solidarity!"

"Huh," I said. It was a monster hill. If I tried it on a bike with fewer than three gears, I usually had to get off and push. But Spencer was a man of action. Research papers were an entirely different undertaking. It was a big ask.

"Or!" Madison bounced a little in her seat. "Even easier—you could just write it for him."

"That would be cheating," Montana told her.

"It would only be cheating if he *won*," she insisted. She looked at me. "Hal, you could write a paper for him that would just, like, count. You wouldn't have to make it good."

"That's ridiculous," Montana declared.

"That could work," I said.

The more I thought about it, the more it seemed like it really could work. If I could get Spencer to agree. And I didn't see any reason why he should. Doing so would screw over his own cousin, probably infuriate his family, and for what? Because the girl who was always yelling at him over the wall asked him to?

And then there was the small matter of the dead koi in his trunk. He still hadn't mentioned it, but it was probably going to be an issue. I wondered why I couldn't have just left a passive-aggressive note under his windshield wiper like a normal person.

Glumly, I concluded that Spencer would probably say no . . . but I still had to ask. It was my only shot.

So, that evening, I stood in my backyard, staring at the wall. There should have been an easier way to get in touch with Spencer, like texting him or knocking on his front door. But I didn't have his number and Spencer's front door lay behind a giant privacy wall with a solid mahogany driveway gate. I didn't fancy explaining myself through an intercom. The wall seemed like the most direct option.

"Hey, pickle, you want pizza?" my dad yelled from inside the house. Friday nights at our house are all about take 'n bake from Valentino's.

"Val's veggie," I called.

"Salad?"

"Nah." I turned back to the wall.

Tonight I wore shorts instead of jeans, which made hopping up on the dock box easier but I scraped my knee on the rough stucco as my feet scrabbled against the wall. Knee stinging, I pulled up on the top and looked down into the Salazars' yard: no Spencer. I dropped back down into my yard and flopped face-up onto the grass. Roundup settled beside me with far more grace and peered at me like, "Now what?"

"I guess I could go try the intercom," I suggested. Like any other person with a solicitation.

Roundup looked completely indifferent.

"Yeah, seems like a lot of effort," I agreed. I'd already put in a full day, arriving at work by six to stock the truck with everything I'd need for the day's assignments, then heading off to Carpinteria to treat a nest of yellow jackets in an outdoor shower. The yellow jackets had been discovered by the owner of the oceanfront beach house when he'd climbed in for a post-surf rinse and slung his wetsuit over the nest. Autumn had labeled the job "URGENT" and the swollen, welted owner had insisted on watching as I doused the nest with insecticide dust followed by an aerosol poison.

For the sake of efficiency, most of our technicians work jobs clustered together, but since I'm in school most of the day, I "float." This means I drive all the hell over the place, and today had been no exception. My second appointment had been on the opposite side of town, in Hope Ranch, where I'd spent half an hour digging though itchy pink insulation in an attic with a three-foot ceiling clearance while searching for a decomposing squirrel corpse. By some miracle, I'd been only seven minutes late to History (still two minutes earlier than Ms. Grijalva) but then I'd discovered Autumn had farmed out my afternoon appointments to other techs and had re-assigned me to help with a house in Goleta where the guys were fumigating for termites.

The hardest part of fumigation is getting the tent (actually a bunch of giant, nylon-coated tarps heat-welded together) secured over a whole house. When you remove a tent, you just kind of stand on the ground and pull and, as long as you don't rip off any rain gutters, you're good to go in a few minutes. Deploying the tent, however, requires lots of measuring and fitting and tall ladders. I had arrived on-site at exactly the wrong moment and found myself scrambling around a rooftop of loose, clay tiles for most of the afternoon. It had been hot and scary and made me yearn for attics full of rotting squirrels.

Yeah, my life pretty much sucks.

Thump.

I lifted my head to see Spencer stepping down off the dock box and onto the grass. I blinked hard. Yep, still there.

Roundup got up, gave him a sniff, and, failing to detect any junk food, wandered into the house.

Spencer strolled over and dropped down beside me. "Hi," he said.

I stared.

"I saw you on the wall and thought you might be looking for me," he explained.

"You saw me?"

"From my window." Spencer gestured at the portion of wall bordering the back of my yard, and his house beyond that. "My room looks out over the pool."

"Just the pool?" I joked. "You don't rate an ocean view?"

"I have windows on that side too."

Of course.

"So were you?" he asked. "Looking for me?"

"I was craving some snacks," I told him.

"I can get you some snacks," he said amiably. "Sweet or savory? We have a wide selection in my pantry."

I giggled. Oh my god, what was that? I was no giggler. "I don't want snacks."

"Doesn't want snacks," he repeated, like he found that slightly shocking. "So, could that mean you were looking for me?"

"Yeah," I admitted.

He gave me an expectant look. I plucked a few blades of grass from the ground and ripped them in half, thinking. Persuasive speaking had never been a strength of mine and this suddenly struck me as the longest of all long shots. A small stack of shredded grass built up on my stomach.

Spencer, beside me, lay back on the lawn and began building his own pile of shredded grass. Finally he offered, "Is it about that thing you mentioned the other day? The scholarship?"

I exhaled gratefully. "Yeah." I turned my head and met his eyes. He was lying awfully close. I felt my heart kick in an extra beat. I really needed to ease up on the caffeine. "I was hoping you'd help."

He gave me a curious look. "What scholarship are we talking about?"

"The Verhaag Scholarship."

His mouth formed a hard line. "Oh, *that* one. The one pushing that crazy rumor about my illustrious great-whatever grandma?"

"Um."

"The one my aunts have been harassing me about every holiday since ninth grade?"

"Well . . . probably."

He gave a curt, unhappy nod. "And you want me to put in a good word for you with the judges," he said, in a cynical tone that seemed strange coming from someone so . . . relaxed.

"No." I sat up. "It's not like that. I can win it on my own. Or, I could have, you know, until . . ." I gave my head a small shake. "Um, no, I want you to apply."

"What?" he asked, still looking annoyed. "Why?"

"Because Britta's applying."

"She is?" he seemed mildly surprised. "Well, then." He gave a small shrug. "She'll win. You probably know how that works. Sorry."

And he did sound genuinely sorry.

"Who the hell is this?" my dad boomed from the backdoor. We both jerked in surprise as he stormed across the yard to glare down at Spencer. "Where did you come from?"

My romantic resume was pretty thin. In second grade, Cooper Diaz had given me a My Little Pony for Valentine's Day and later kissed my cheek while we'd been filling the milk order. But, a week later, I'd told the teacher on him for stealing my SpongeBob pencil and, in retaliation, he'd socked me in the stomach at recess. To this day, if I thought about it long enough, I could almost feel the intense pain in my belly and the lumpy, acidic feel of half-digested goldfish in the back of my throat. That had been pretty much it for elementary school.

Middle school had been an unfortunate time for me. I'd worn braces almost twice as long as necessary because my parents had always been fighting over who should pay for them or take me to the appointments and the one thing my parents *had* agreed on— though for entirely different reasons—was that I was not allowed to shave my legs. Middle school had passed with no action.

High school might have been different—the braces were gone and I'd declared agency over my own leg hair in the spring of eighth grade—but I'd been really busy. I'd almost made some time for Logan Holmes when he'd asked me out last year, but he'd wanted to take me to a polo match, which had brought back memories of Cooper and his pony-theft-abuse cycle. I'd passed and Logan moved on to Cassandra Hattenbach. They made a very nice couple.

Anyway, my dad had never had to contemplate the abstract concept of me going on a date, much less confront the presence of a real, live teenage boy on his property. Men like my dad were glaciers. You had to ease them into these things, giving them plenty of time and carbon emissions. I needed to defuse the situation before he had a cardiac event. "This is Spencer. He delivers snacks."

"Oh, yeah?" he demanded. "Where are the snacks? Why isn't he wearing a shirt? And what are you doing to my grass!"

We were saved by the oven timer. Spencer opted to stay and help us eat the pizzas, which revealed him to be a far braver boy than I'd ever given him credit for. My dad was not at all pleased to learn Spencer lived next door. I could totally see why this shocked him—Spencer had only lived there for *seventeen years*. Dad muttered something about razor wire and accused Roundup of dereliction of duty. I quickly dished pizza onto two plates and led Spencer back out into the yard, giving my dad the same look I used to make Roundup get off the couch. My dad glared and headed toward the living room with his plate.

We settled onto the grass, ignoring the patio table, and I dug into my slice.

"All right. Explain to me about the scholarship," Spencer said.

I swallowed my bite. "There's a provision in the rules," I said. "If two of your family members apply, judging defaults to a panel of people unaffiliated with the Verhaag Foundation."

He gave a short, surprised laugh. "Really?"

I nodded. "It's kind of buried in the back of the rulebook, but it's there."

Spencer, still grinning, ate a few more bites of pizza. I got up and went into the house, returning with two fresh slices, and dumped one onto Spencer's plate. We nommed. Finally he said, "So you're asking me to apply for a scholarship I don't want so that this rule applies and judging is taken away from my family, so that you win the scholarship instead of my cousin."

When he put it like that it sounded kind of bad.

"I just want a fair shot at it," I defended. "I've been working on this paper for three years. Three. Years. I work two jobs so I can save up for living expenses. I've already applied early action to Georgetown. My whole life depends on getting this scholarship."

"Your whole life?" He raised an eyebrow.

"Yes," I said seriously. "My whole life."

Spencer set down his plate, brushed his hands together, and stood up. "I'll think about it," he said. Then he stepped onto the dock box and hoisted himself over the wall.

"Thanks for the pizza," he called from the other side.

I lay back in the grass and stared up at the cloudless sky, trying not to imagine four more years of this same view.

Later that night, a knock on the glass slider to my bedroom woke me from a deep sleep. I rolled over, switched on the lamp, and gaped at the sight of Spencer lounging on the other side of the screen.

"Are you sleeping?" He looked stunned.

"Yes!"

"It's nine o'clock."

"I get up early," I said, grabbing at the sheets.

"Cute shirt," he commented. "I like the dolphins."

Oh my god. "What do you want, Spencer?"

"I need to see those scholarship forms. If that thing about the judging is true," he said, "I'll do it."

CHAPTER 6

I knew he would do it!" Madison squealed. She turned to Spencer, who sat with his cheek propped on his palm, carefully reading through the scholarship application packet. "I knew you would do it!"

It was ten a.m. and the three of us sat on the curb in front of my house. A cyclist dinged his bell angrily and swerved out of the bike lane to avoid our feet.

We weren't obstructing the bike lane to be difficult. Moments before, we had been sitting in my front yard, well out of everyone's way . . . until my dad looked out and noticed us squashing his beloved grass. Lawn maintenance was his god and, apparently, the front yard was his temple. The words, "Get off my lawn!" had actually come out of his mouth.

We moved.

I tucked my feet as close to the curb as I could get them and studied Spencer as he perused the application requirements. His damp hair stuck out at funny angles and the dried salt crystals on his cheek glinted in the morning light. The zig-zag imprints left by his wetsuit seams were visible on his bare shoulders, neck, and wrists. His shoes matched his shirt.

"Won't your mom be mad?" Madison asked.

"Nah," he said, turning the page, "we mostly avoid her side of the family. Might see them at Thanksgiving but they'll probably have forgotten by then." That seemed optimistic to me but I kept my mouth shut. He flipped back to the previous page and began rereading the section on content requirements.

"Look, you don't have to worry about the research paper," I told him. "I really, really appreciate you doing this. I'll write the paper for you. I know you're not—"

Spencer's head came up. "That would be cheating."

I turned to Madison and motioned for her to jump in. It almost made sense when she explained it.

"Nope. It would be cheating if you used the paper she writes you to *win*," she stressed, "but that's not going to happen. Hal's been working on her paper for years. She could probably, like, get it published in some smarty-pants college journal if anyone actually cared about this Gold Rush guy. You're just going to turn in something that satisfies the requirements so Hal has a fair shot."

"I've got a lot of unused material," I said. "I can put together something for you to submit pretty quickly. It won't be great but it'll qualify as an entry."

Spencer gave me an annoyed look. "I can write my own submission."

"The paper has to be twenty-five pages," I pointed out, "with parenthetical citations."

"I see that."

"The submission period ends next week." I'd turned in my paper almost two months ago.

"I've got this."

"Spencer . . ."

"Don't worry about it, Hal. I said I'd do it. I got this." He got to his feet and tucked the papers under his arm. "I'll see you guys later." He balanced along the curb until he reached his driveway, punched a code into the security pad, and pushed through the gate.

"At least take my notes!" I called after him.

He waved his hand over his head dismissively and the gate clicked shut behind him.

I turned to Madison with the beginnings of panic on my face.

"Oof. That went all wrong at the end," she observed. "Do you want his email? You could go ahead and send him your notes. Just in case." I nodded and she pulled out her phone and tapped on the screen. "So . . . Plan B?"

"There is no Plan B." Plan B implied a reasonable alternative. The best I had was damage control which, in this case, meant stacking my extracurricular deck so as to qualify for the Santa Barbara Promise. Maybe I could transfer to a UC after two years. It would have to be UCSB or Cal Poly, though. I'd managed to save up a nice chunk of change but UCSB still cost fourteen grand a year. I'd have to live at home. With my dad. Killing bugs between classes. And, oh yeah, changing diapers on my nights off. I dropped my face into my hands. There had to be other options. French Foreign Legion? I wasn't French. Was the Merchant Marine still a thing? Even if it was, they probably cared about extracurriculars too.

I described my failed attempt to join yearbook staff to Madison.

"Montana and I are joining the sailing team," she offered. "Maybe you could too."

Well, at least that would appeal to the Merchant Marine. "You don't know how to sail," I observed.

"No, but the sailing people say they can teach us. They're

super nice. The team captain is really excited about how much we weigh. I guess a light crew makes the boat go faster."

"Not all of us weigh ninety pounds with shoes on," I said. "And learning to sail sounds time-consuming."

"Yeah," Madison agreed, "but we get to see seals, and whales, and dolphins." She closed her eyes and scrunched her shoulders in ecstasy. "I love dolphins."

Montana came out the front door of their house and crossed the street, yawning, her hair twisted up in a floppy bun. She held a Pop-Tart in one hand and a Diet Coke in the other.

"Good morning," she said. "What are we talking about?"

"Tell me that's not your breakfast," Madison said.

Montana toasted her sister with her breakfast pastry. "Health."

"We're talking about extracurriculars," I said.

"That again?"

"It's damage control. Do you think backgammon club sounds like a legit extracurricular?"

"What, are you ninety?" Montana asked, at the same time Madison said, "Nope."

I sighed.

Montana took a big glug of Diet Coke and asked, "What happened to yearbook?"

Her sister launched into the tale of my failed yearbook career, somehow making the telling last twice as long as mine had. My mind began to wander. I contemplated going inside to get my own Diet Coke.

"I think you should do it," Montana announced.

"What, backgammon club?"

"Just have a look around his yard. If there's a shed or any-thing, maybe take a little peek inside."

"What are you—" I gaped at her. "Do you mean Tyler Lofaro's yard? Are you serious right now? Do you want me to go to jail?"

"Please. Take your extendable toilet brush thingy—"

"It's not a toilet brush," I said. It just kind of looked like one.

"—and walk around dusting the spider webs off their roof and whatever else you do with it. No one will even notice you."

"Yes, they w—"

She cut me off. "So, suppose someone does bust you? Oops, you've got the wrong address. No one's going to complain about free spiderweb removal."

"That's ridiculous," I said. I turned to Madison for backup. I should have known better.

"Tyler Lofaro's a dick," she said, nodding earnestly. "Go search his house."

My friends were ridiculous. And persistent. I was relieved when the time came to get ready for work. I left Madison and Montana on the curb plotting felonies, escaped into my house, forwarded all my notes to Spencer, and changed into my uniform.

Saturdays I work the lunch shift at Caddysnack, a miniature-golf-and-small-plates "dining experience" located just north of town. If you want to putt golf balls through wine country–themed hazards while juggling a plate of ahi tuna sliders, Caddysnack is your place. We have a full bar, so there's usually quite a crowd on Friday and Saturday nights. Afternoons, not so much. I typi-cally earn minimum wage and I do it wearing tight golf knickers, argyle knee socks, an undersized sweater vest, and a newsboy cap. It's like *The Legend of Bagger Vance* attacked a Hooters waitress.

My dad does not like this job—at all—but my mom signed

off on the work permit for it, citing her conviction that waitressing is a valuable life skill. I guess she would know.

Being seventeen and too young to legally serve alcohol, my official title is bus girl. Most of the time it's me, the bartender, and one server working the day shift. If things get busy, I pitch in serving, and if someone orders alcohol, the bartender walks it over. This doesn't happen all that often but today looked like it could be one of those days. I was pleased at the prospect of earning some tips for once, but Monica, the server working with me, didn't seem so sure.

"It's a bachelor party, kiddo, and they're pretty obnoxious. Maybe I should call Ethan and see if he can get someone else to come in."

Sergio, the bartender, snorted. "Yeah, that'll happen." Our manager, Ethan, liked to keep costs low by understaffing. We all knew he'd never call someone in on a Saturday afternoon.

"Don't worry," Sergio told Monica, "I'll keep an eye on her."

Monica looked apprehensive but handed me a tray piled with baskets of tempura green beans and sriracha aioli to deliver. I sallied forth and found the bachelor party by the second hole, a meandering path through artificial grape vines and quaint sections of weathered fencing. About half of them had already taken their shots and moved along to wait by the hole, which was on the other side of a stack of wine barrels. I handed out green beans to waiting golfers and backed away while they tried to figure out the trick to putting while holding a beer and a piping hot snack basket. (Had they asked I could have told them: there is no trick. Ever seen Tiger Woods holding a plate of nachos on the back nine? Nope.)

I wished them luck, left a big stack of napkins for them on

a fake rock, and hurried back to the order window to report to Monica.

"Did that go okay?" she asked anxiously.

"No problem," I assured her.

She looked relieved. "I just checked in another big group. It's a birthday party and they didn't bother to call ahead. I've gotta get them clubs and take their drink order. Can you run the rest of these apps to group one? Tell them I'll be right behind you to check on their drinks."

"Sure." I looked out at the course. A lattice wall partially blocked my view but lots of loud cheering from over by the busing station indicated the bachelor party had progressed to hole three. I grabbed another round of baskets off the counter and made my way over. As I came around the lattice, I realized the loud cheering had nothing to do with their golf game.

Standing by the cart of glass ketchup bottles was none other than Tyler Lofaro. I watched as Tyler hoisted one of the bottles, *licked* the rim, screwed on the cap, and placed it back amongst the rows of identical red bottles. His buddies lost it and he reached for another.

"*Hey,*" I said loudly.

As is common practice in fine dining establishments, ketchup bottles at Caddysnack are never replaced. When the levels of ketchup in the bottles runs low, we top them up from a big plastic vat of (off-brand) ketchup, wipe them clean, and put them back in circulation.

There was no way to know which—or how many—bottles Tyler had just contaminated with his entitled bro-cooties. We would have to recycle the whole cart and I could only imagine Ethan's reaction to that. He would probably charge me for them.

Tyler looked up with an expression of evil delight. "Oh, hell, it's bug girl!" He set down the ketchup and picked up his putter and his drink, which happened to be a beer. I checked his wrist and, sure enough, he was wearing one of the blue bands we give to customers over twenty-one. This practice makes it easy to identify who is legal to serve when multiple waitstaff are working and to get one you have to show an ID. No exceptions. Ethan is paranoid and makes us card absolutely everyone, even on Senior Tuesdays.

I considered calling him on it but any challenge from me was bound to have an adverse effect on Monica's tip.

"Hey, bug girl, did you hear me?"

So here's the thing about food service: all of the normal routes to the high road are blocked with a giant "detour or be fired" sign. You don't get to ignore people. You don't get to make smartass comments. (Okay, maybe that isn't the high road, but it always makes me feel better.) You basically just have to take the abuse and smile and hope people are still feeling satisfied and superior when it comes time to pay the check. This is not a career path for people concerned with human dignity. If I weren't so desperate to get away from my parents, I would've quit halfway through my first day.

I turned and said, "Hi, Tyler. Can I get you anything?" The smile I gave him was more like a flash of clenched teeth but the offer sounded passably sincere. Maybe.

"Yeah," he said. He took a step toward me, staggering a little as he left the supporting ketchup cart behind. "You can effing stay away from my car and my yearbook staff. You're an effing *pest*."

Here's the point where I realized this was not Tyler's first beer.

"Can I get you some onion rings?" I offered. "You seem like you could use some onion rings." I deserve credit for that, right? That was super nice of me. Above and beyond.

"Screw you!" Tyler screamed, spraying my face with a fine mist of beery spittle.

"Whoa, dude." The other guys in Tyler's party, all of whom looked old enough to swill their beers legally, had stopped giggling long enough to notice their underaged buddy was having a meltdown. One of them walked over and threw an arm around Tyler's shoulders. Another eased the putter from Tyler's hand. They let him keep the beer.

"I'll be back in a few minutes to check on you," I said cheerfully. "Wave if you need anything."

I marched back to the bar and scrubbed my face with a clean bar mop and half a bottle of hand sanitizer. I briefly hesitated, concerned for Monica's tip, but they were all drinking Coors Light. Statistically speaking, Coors Light drinkers were the very worst tippers.

"Hey, Sergio?" I addressed Sergio's back, as he was busy cleaning the frozen margarita machine.

"Yes, my dear?"

"That guy over there? The one foaming at the mouth and spilling his beer all over the tractor hazard?"

"Uh huh?"

"He's in my class. In high school."

Monica swore she had checked Tyler's ID but, with a huge party waiting on her at the check-in counter, she hadn't examined it closely. I was pretty sure her tip died the second she informed the bachelor party that Sergio was calling the cops. Tyler left like his pants were on fire but his hostility had already rubbed off on his companions, who played six more passive-aggressive holes before demanding the check. None of us were surprised when they stiffed us on the tip.

I apologetically handed my meager afternoon earnings over to Monica, who took them after token protest. I left work feeling harassed and penniless, only to find someone had flung a ramekin of sriracha aioli across my windshield.

I stomped back inside to the busing station, dumped the empty dish into one of the plastic bus bins, and snatched up some cleaning supplies. I returned to the truck and used bar mops to squeegee off as much of the greasy, pink sludge as possible, then poured a few pitchers of water over my windshield wipers. As I worked, I fantasized about drowning Tyler Lofaro in a vat of expired mayo. Finally, I hauled everything back inside and trudged out to my truck feeling so completely over this day, this week, and particularly this job.

My clean-up efforts had created a milky, pinkish puddle of aioli juice beneath the front of the truck, which I was careful to step around as I rooted in my backpack for my keys. Thus distracted, it was not until I rounded the hood that I discovered her, battered and dangling by one leg, her other legs mangled and smashed. Below her, on the asphalt, lay an abandoned putter.

"Shelob!" I cried.

I lunged forward, dropping my backpack, and cradled her in my arms, but with one of her legs still bolted to the truck, I couldn't lift her down. I gently eased her back against the truck and pulled my tool kit out of the truck box. Sergio took his break and came out and held my spider while I painstakingly detached the last leg. Together, we loaded Shelob into the truck bed and secured her with some bungee cord.

"You saw he beat up the side of the truck some too?" Sergio asked gently.

"I saw."

"We really should have called the cops on that little fuck," he mused.

"Don't worry," I told him. "I'll take care of it."

CHAPTER 7

I decided the safest time to search Tyler's house would be right after he left for school in the morning. Doing it then would make me blatantly late—I'd have to take a tardy—but thanks to Ms. Grijalva's on-going love fest with Coach Bell, I had tardies to spare.

Tyler's family lived in an enormous Victorian in Upper East, just a few blocks from the high school. I'd pulled his address from our files—his family did, in fact, have a service agreement with MPC—and waited down the block until I saw the gray Tesla roll out of the driveway and speed silently off in the direction of school. He could have walked there in less time than it would take him to find two parking spaces to hog but I guessed if you had a Tesla, you could drive to your own mailbox without feeling guilty.

I was driving one of the company's spare vehicles, a white Ford Transit Connect my dad had bought at auction. Dad never bothered to have a logo wrap put on it, which I thought might be an advantage if I was going to drive around breaking the law. There were probably a hundred white work vans just like it puttering anonymously through the streets of Santa Barbara. Paired with my MPC polo shirt, the van provided the perfect suburban camouflage. But the paneled windows ruined my visibility and it smelled of stale fried chicken. Alas, Johan at the auto body shop estimated repairs to Shelob and my Ranger would take at least a week.

Recalling the damage to my spider quelled my nervousness. I nosed the Transit into Tyler's drive and parked in one of the guest spots. As I unloaded my pesticide tank and telescoping round brush, one of the garage doors rolled open and a yacht-like Mercedes pulled out, a middle-aged man—Tyler's dad, presumably—at the wheel. The garage door slid back down. The man waved and drove off.

Wow, so far this was really easy.

I got to work circling the house, brushing spider webs and the beginnings of bird nests off the eaves and lower roofs. When I reached the backyard I found a garden shed, a pool house, and a smallish, square structure, all unlocked. I made a big show of pulling out my tank and spray wand as I checked each, pacing the foundations as if I were laying down lines of pesticide. The garden shed held holiday decorations; the pool house held couches, a bathroom, and a foosball table; and the flat wooden structure held the pump and filtration machinery for the pool and spa. None of them held two thousand yearbook supplements.

I turned my gaze to the big house, with its fish-scale siding and steep gables. I imagined a house like that would have several handy-dandy attic spaces for the concealment of stolen goods. I wasn't getting inside without a service call, though. I was pondering the feasibility of planting some live ants by the foundation when a woman exited through the french doors and stomped toward me.

"Hey!" she called out.

I froze.

"Do you even *see* the pergola?"

"I'm sorry?"

"The one you walked right under without brushing the beams? Again. Last time you people came out, you completely ignored the entire loggia. I'm having a party on Friday and I had better not see a single spider out here or I'm taking my business to Terminix."

I resumed breathing. "Yes, ma'am. I'll go over all the beams." Then, because why not, I offered, "I'm sure you've heard about the ant problems in this area. While I'm here, are you experiencing any issues?"

Mrs. Lofaro gave me a dissatisfied look. "Issues? Like what?"

"We've been seeing a lot of carpenter ant infestations in attics in this neighborhood." Wow. I was really good at this. I was starting to scare myself.

"We don't have attics. Our second floor ceilings are vaulted." She wrinkled her nose at my insinuation her house might possess something as plebeian as an attic.

"Oh. That's good." Well, Leah could cross that off her list. I turned to start on the columns of the pergola, which shaded a large outdoor seating area.

"But we do have a basement. Maybe you should check it."

As old houses went, the Lofaros had one of the better basements I'd seen: dry, updated wiring and systems, no sign of recent termite activity . . . and definitely no yearbook supplements. No anything, really. The low ceiling height, dim lighting, and exposed ductwork clearly discouraged the Lofaros from coming down here. Mrs. Lofaro hadn't even descended the stairs to show me the light switch.

This had been a colossal waste of time, and after my thorough scrubbing of the loggia and my basement inspection, I was beyond tardy. I'd be lucky to make first period at all.

I climbed back up the stairs to the kitchen where Mrs. Lofaro waited impatiently, arms crossed. I was beginning to see where Tyler got his charming personality. "Looks good," I said with a polite smile. "We'll have a technician out for your next service treatment in three months. Have a great day."

"Wait," Mrs. Lofaro ordered, handing me a slip of paper. "This is the address of one of our rental properties. It's been vacant a few months and we have a new tenant moving in, a single woman." She rolled her eyes, like she found the idea of unmarried women in houses completely absurd. "We don't have a service contract on that property but I need it sprayed for bugs before I have the carpets cleaned. I don't want to give this woman a reason to complain about anything. Can you handle that or do I need to call your manager?"

A whole other property? One that had been vacant for months?

I took the paper. "Oh, yes ma'am, I can take care of that. Would you like me to write you an estimate?"

I was very late indeed but I'd found a real lead and, feeling all detective-y, I accepted my tardy with good cheer. I recapped everything for Montana before Virtual Enterprise and we high-fived. "You're like Veronica Mars, but with roaches," she said.

"I'd settle for Inspector Gadget. I just want to find those supplements."

"You're going to nail that little jerk," she said confidently.

I was starting to think I might. Next I tracked down Leah and filled her in.

"Do you think they're in there?" she asked excitedly.

I shrugged. "It sounds promising."

"I'm coming with you," she declared.

"Ha. No, you're not."

"I can help!"

"I'm a pest control technician, I drive a truck full of poison," I said patiently. "I don't do ride-alongs. Company policy."

Okay, so there's no company policy regarding ride-alongs. We don't need one because no one ever wants to ride along. But I had my usual number of appointments lined up and I wouldn't be able to skip out on those without somehow clearing it with Autumn. Lemmethinkaboutit—no. My plan was to handle it after I finished my scheduled jobs, which would put me at the Lofaros' place kind of late. I had a signed estimate officially hiring me for this job but it still seemed wise to avoid doing anything that might make the neighbors take notice. Leah, with her blue hair and cherry red Velma glasses, wasn't exactly subtle.

"Fine. FaceTime me when you get there," she ordered. "I want to make sure you don't miss anything."

"I'll text you after if I find anything," I told her firmly and made my escape before she got any more ideas.

My afternoon appointments took longer than expected, due in large part to the last-minute addition of a follow-up visit to the rat-infested guest cottage in Montecito. I wished I knew why they kept requesting me specifically so I could do something to lose that privilege, but I dutifully went out and baited the traps I'd placed the week before, scattering extra bait in a wide circle while Irma supervised from the bottom of the attic stairs. Despite a week in the attic, my traps looked undisturbed, so I wasn't too concerned they'd catch anything. Even supposing they did, this would only work once. You can catch mice in traps all day long, but rats are smart. As soon as one of them disappears, the rest start to wonder, Hey, where's Bob? and then you still have an attic full of rats, but now they're *suspicious* rats. I anticipated little to no rat disposal in my future, and my irritation had mellowed by the time I handed Irma another invoice. My dad didn't pay me overtime but an extra hour on the clock never hurt.

When I finished in Montecito, it was late enough that I decided I'd better go home and let the dog out before heading to the Lofaro rental. Roundup ran outside for a lightning pee, then bolted back into the house, attaching himself to my hip. He gave me a tortured look as I headed for the front door.

"I'd take you with me if I could," I explained, shoving him back with my knee. "I'm driving this stupid van and there's no way to keep you out of the cargo area. You might get into the chemicals."

Roundup gave a despondent moan.

"Dad will be home soon," I promised, closing the door most of the way, then easing my leg out. Roundup gave a loud shriek to trick me into thinking I'd shut his nose in the door, which I ignored. I locked the deadbolt and turned, nearly colliding with Spencer Salazar. I jerked back, startled, and the back of my head hit the front door with a *thunk*. Roundup reacted with a panicked bark.

"Why are you on my porch?" I demanded. The door shuddered at my back as Roundup launched himself against the other side of it. "Roundup, chill!"

Spencer gave me a patient look. "I'm coming to see you."

Upon hearing the voice of Spencer the Snack King, Roundup settled and I moved away from the door. "Well, I've got to go."

"Didn't you just get home?"

"One more job," I told him.

"Okay," he said, "I'll tag along."

Seriously? Why did everyone suddenly want to be an assistant pest control technician? "No."

"Why not?"

So many reasons. I settled on: "You're not wearing a shirt."

"I have shirts."

"Do you?"

Spencer ignored that. "I'll be right back. Don't go anywhere."

Five minutes later Spencer got into the van wearing, as promised, a shirt. Sort of. Well, I guess I hadn't specified sleeves. To be fair, if anyone should've been running around town in shirts without sleeves, it was Spencer. He had killer arms. Not thick but defined—the kind of arms you got from lots and lots of paddling out through the surf. And . . . ugh, why was I thinking about Spencer's arms? I gave my head a shake and started the van.

"So, whose vermin are we going to poison? Anyone I know?"

"It's a rental." I hesitated, then admitted, "Belonging to the Lofaros."

"Why," Spencer turned to me with an amazed look on his face, "would you want to go anywhere near Tyler Lofaro?"

Spencer had heard all about my encounter with Tyler on Saturday. Madison's bedroom window faces the street and, as soon as she'd realized I'd arrived home spiderless, she'd grabbed Montana and hustled over. I'd been standing with them in my driveway, still dressed in my stupid golf knickers, when Spencer had emerged from his compound.

"I can't believe that little troll," Montana had fumed. "You should have called the cops."

"For some reason, my employers frown on the name of their

establishment appearing in the Police Beat," I told her. "Besides, I have no proof. He was gone by the time I got out there and there aren't any cameras on the employee lot."

"You should have your mom call his mom!" Madison declared, outraged.

Montana and I just looked at her.

"This isn't dance team," Montana said finally.

I had been about to say, "This isn't third grade," but perhaps the differences between those two institutions were subtle.

"What happened to your spider?" Spencer asked, coasting into my driveway on his skateboard.

Madison cast a pitiful glance in my direction. "I think she's going to need a new one."

"No way," I insisted. "Shelob can't be killed with a putter. She guards the stairs to Mordor. She drinks the blood of Elves and Men!" I ignored their stares and nodded confidently. "The body shop can fix her."

We all studied the splintered pile of fiberglass in the truck bed.

"They can fix her," I said again. "Right?"

"I don't know, sweetie," Montana said, "does Doc McStuffins work there?"

I looked at her helplessly.

"Who's going to tell me what happened to the spider?" Spencer asked calmly.

Montana then decided to spill the *whole* story, including the parts about the parking wars and the missing yearbook supplements. Spencer had vehemently agreed with Montana—that I should call the police—and also with my dad—that I should quit that job.

Like anybody had asked him.

So now, as we drove over to the Lofaros' rental property, I

could sense Spencer getting worked up all over again, and I was going to have to listen to it because we were already too far from home for me to throw him out of the van.

"Seriously, Spencer, don't worry about it. I'm not going near Tyler," I told him. "I'm going to a property owned by his parents which, for all I know, Tyler has never set foot in."

Spencer's face was incredulous. "Why?"

"I'm looking for the yearbook supplements."

"Again . . . why?"

"Because. I need to join yearbook."

"No, you don't. I agreed to apply for the scholarship, remember? And I'm drafting my submission—which I do not need your notes to accomplish, although they looked very . . . thorough. I hope you don't mind if I forward them to someone who might actually need them. And I'm not even going to open that other attachment you sent because, like I said, I can and will write my *own* submission. That's taken care of. The way you and the twins tell it, all you have to do now is wait for the awards ceremony and practice your acceptance speech."

My phone chimed with an incoming text. I was at a light, so I risked a quick glance at the screen. Mom.

"Am I missing something?" Spencer asked. "Maybe you just want to get him busted for assaulting your spider? I told you, you need to call the police. Revenge is never a good plan. Weren't you paying attention when we read *The Iliad* last year?"

I rolled my eyes. "I'm not Achilles. I'm just trying to help a friend and get on yearbook staff. It's called damage control."

"What damage are you controlling for? I—" Spencer broke off as my phoned chimed with three texts in quick succession.

"I—" It chimed again.

"Does it always do that?" he asked, distracted.

"Yes," I answered shortly.

He gave my phone a wary look and tried again. "You told me your paper is going to dominate."

"It will—if it makes it in front of real judges."

"Okay, so, what am I missing? All of this, " he waved a hand vaguely, "was your idea."

"It's just in case," I told him.

Spencer pivoted toward me as much as the seat belt would allow and stared at me for a long moment. "You don't think I can do it."

"Hmm?" I pulled up in front of a small craftsman cottage and checked the address against the paper Mrs. Lofaro had given me.

"You don't think I can handle writing my own submission."

Duh. "It's due in two days, Spencer."

The look he gave me was equal parts offense and annoyance. "I said I'd get it done. In fact, that's what I was coming over to talk to you about." He waved a folded section of newsprint at me. I hadn't noticed him carrying anything. Where had he put it?

I squinted at the moving paper, trying to read the header. "*The New York Times?*"

"Yeah," he said, "I found this article about some islands the US owns way out in the Pacific. They've been declared a national monument and they're just exploding with wildlife, like sea turtles, and giant clams, and boobies—"

"What!"

"It's a kind of bird. It's got blue feet. Anyway, back in the nineteenth century, these islands were known forrr . . ." he drew the word out, building suspense, "guano mining."

"Bat poo."

"Bird poo," he corrected.

I opened the van door and got out. Bird poo. Ohh-kay.

"Doesn't it remind you of all that Gold Rush stuff Robert W. Service wrote about?"

I glared at him for a beat. "*What* are you . . . ? You know what? Never mind. I've gotta find those supplements."

"Hal." Spencer got out on his side and faced me across the hood. "I'll get it done, I promise. Forget about Tyler. Or don't forget about Tyler, and call the cops. But leave this yearbook thing alone. That kid is a maniac."

"I have to work," I told him.

Spencer's mouth firmed. "I'm coming in with you."

Whatever. I unstrapped my insecticide tank from the back of the van, marched up the little stone pathway and punched the code Mrs. Lofaro had given me into the front door.

Spencer followed me into the abbreviated entryway and did a slow spin, taking it all in. "Wow, this is a lot of carpet."

"Places always look weird without furniture," I told him, using my wand to lay down a line of Cy-kick spray along the lefthand baseboard.

He disappeared down the hall and returned less than a minute later. "I don't see any yearbook supplements."

That figured.

Spencer continued to wander around. "They left their TV."

The TV was the size of a sheet of plywood. "Probably too big to get through the door."

"Do you think the cable's on?"

"Why don't you go check? Please."

Spencer moved over to the living area and began fiddling with the TV. "So why would someone hire you to spray a vacant house? I don't see any roaches or anything."

"Mmm." I shrugged and continued my circuit, spraying as I went. "It's a pretty common precaution for rental units. Bugs are funny. Some of them can lie dormant for months until something stimulates them. Like rollie pollies. Well, they're not actually insects, but did you know they can live—"

I glanced over at Spencer and almost dropped my tank. He stood in front of the enormous flat-screen TV with a remote in his hand. Beneath his feet, the dark, earth-toned carpet boiled with movement. I blinked. Thousands of tiny black dots seethed and frothed toward Spencer in a voracious wave.

"Out!" I shouted. "Out, out, out!"

I immediately followed my own advice, sprinting for the door. Behind me, I heard Spencer muttering, "What the . . ."

I dashed to the van, snatched the can of OFF! Deep Woods from my go-kit in the back, and sprayed it liberally over my shoes and pant legs. I gave my lower extremities a quick inspection, then turned to look back at the house. Spencer still hadn't come out.

"Spencer!" I yelled. I sat down in the front seat of the van to do a more thorough check of my ankles. "Spencer, get out here now!"

A loud curse came from within the cottage. Seconds later, Spencer appeared in the doorway, grabbing spastically at the legs of his jeans. I dropped the can of OFF! on the sidewalk—hey, I left it out there for him, okay, so don't judge me—swung my legs into the van, and shut the door.

Spencer ran up to the passenger door, his expression wild with panic. "They're all over me! Hal!"

My eyes met his beautiful gray ones through the window while my hand felt for the button on the inside of the door.

"Bummer," I said with feeling, and engaged the lock.

CHAPTER 8

After a brief search, Spencer found a garden hose in the backyard and was able to strip and rinse off. At my insistence, he threw his clothes in the outside trashcan and I gave him a new Tyvek suit to wear, fresh out of the package. My dad rationed those things like gold and the next time I had to slog through a crawl space, I'd probably be doing it in my street clothes. Spencer did not appear to appreciate my sacrifice.

"Fleas are really weird," I said, breaking the heavy silence in the van as we drove home through the darkening streets. "A flea pupa can lie dormant for a really long time if it doesn't have a host nearby. But as soon as it senses heat or movement, it pops out of its cocoon," I snapped my fingers, "ready to eat."

"Fascinating," Spencer ground out.

"So, I guess there were some pupal fleas—" maybe the biggest freaking swarm I'd ever seen, "—hanging out in that carpet. Maybe the last renter had pets."

He stared straight ahead.

I shrugged and focused on driving. I wasn't going to feel guilty. Nope, I wasn't. I hadn't asked him to come along. In fact, I had actively discouraged him. Why had he wanted to come along, anyway? To talk about guano mining? He was supposed to be working on his research paper. And now, with my luck, he'd get typhus from all those flea bites and be too sick to write his paper. And the CDC would show up, and guess who would get blamed for the epidemic?

I risked a glance at Spencer. His arms were crossed over his chest and he was fidgeting his feet and legs in quick little micro taps, probably trying not to scratch them.

With a sigh I offered, "Buy you a taco?"

I bought him three tacos and a large horchata. Okay, so maybe I was feeling a little guilty. Then I ordered myself a fried avocado torta because guilt makes me hungry. We got our food to go and ate it in Spencer's yard, sitting on the lounge chairs by the pool. Spencer had consumed all three tacos in about a minute and a half and now reclined on the pool chaise sucking down his drink.

"How come you're always out here by the pool?" I asked him as I finished the last bite of my sandwich. "You must have pretty killer views from the backyard."

Spencer indicated the pool area with a tilt of his head. "Quieter here. My parents are in the backyard a lot with their friends. There's an outdoor kitchen and stuff back there."

We sat in peaceful silence, contemplating the pool. It was a really nice pool, with one of those flat, shallow areas you lie around on and a hot tub that overflowed on purpose, cascading into the pool with a soothing tinkle.

"I'm sorry about the fleas," I told him. "I shouldn't have let you come with me."

"No-o-o, you shouldn't have locked me out of the car." His voice grew kind of loud by the end of that sentence.

"Then we'd both have fleas," I said reasonably.

Spencer exhaled. "Look, if I *swear* to you I will turn in a submission by the deadline, will you please stay away from Tyler Lofaro's house? Hous*es*? Especially that flea-ridden rental?"

I gave him a skeptical look. "An *eligible* submission? By Wednesday?"

"Yes. If mine isn't ready, I'll turn in the one you sent me. But I won't need to."

I doubted Robert Service himself could write a research paper of that length by Wednesday, much less Spencer. It didn't seem politic to say so, however, and I had nothing to lose by promising. I'd already searched Tyler's house and the flea-shack.

"Deal," I said.

"Good." Spencer set his drink down and sat up, facing me. His expression changed. "Do you want to go for a swim?"

I stretched my neck, suddenly feeling strangely restless. "Um . . ."

"The spa is on too," he added.

Okay, that was a terrible idea. Essay or no essay, I would not be spending flirty pool time with a guy who'd been successfully torturing me from across the property line for almost a decade. Even if he did look like a young surf god in the evening light.

"Sure," I heard myself say. "I'll go put on a swimsuit."

"Want a boost over the wall?"

We both glanced behind us at the wall separating our yards. I shook my head. "I can't unlock the slider from the outside. I have to walk around."

"I'll walk with you," he offered. He stood and grabbed my hand, using it to hoist me to my feet.

"Okay," I agreed uncertainly as he towed me away from the pool and past the front of his house, and turned down the driveway. One of the garage doors rolled up and Spencer's mom pulled out of it driving his black BMW. We stepped onto the gravel border to give her room to pass. She gave us a friendly wave and called, "Back in a bit!" through the open window while she waited for the gate to open. Then she turned left onto Bluff Drive and was gone.

I stared after her. "Why is your mom driving your car?"

"That's her car," Spencer informed me. "I borrowed it a couple times while she was out of town."

My breath seized in my lungs.

"Polly and I used to share the Volvo," he continued, referring to his older sister, "but she took it to college with her. My dad and I have gone car shopping a few times but I haven't really seen anything I like yet. Hey, what's wrong?"

"When's the last time you drove your mom's car?" I demanded.

"I don't know. Last week, maybe? I usually take my dad's Land Cruiser."

I wrapped my arms around my middle and stared at Spencer in horror.

"Hallie, what?"

"I thought you were just a really good sport," I said faintly.

"Well, sure, I guess," he replied, sounding mystified. "I mean, I don't remember anyone ever saying otherwise."

I had to tell him. Considering Spencer's evening so far had featured an attack by pestilent insects and a frenzied soak in a frigid garden hose, I wouldn't have blamed him if he'd chosen that moment to completely freak out on me. Instead he listened very calmly, and even laughed at one point. Nervously.

He really was a good sport.

He took a deep breath. "So, to recap, there's a dead fish in my mom's trunk, and it's been there for almost a week?"

"Yes," I confirmed.

"Okay." He walked purposefully to the nearest door, opened it, and yelled, "Hey, Dad! Where'd Mom go?"

I was too far away to hear the whole answer but I did catch the word "groceries."

Spencer and I shared a frantic look and leapt into action.

"I'll get the spare keys." He disappeared into the house.

"I'll get the odor spray," I said to no one.

He met me at the end of my driveway in a gray Toyota SUV. I dove into the passenger seat and Spencer took off down the street before I'd closed the door all the way.

"It's in a trash bag," I said. "Maybe it won't be too bad."

Spencer didn't reply.

The first place we checked was the neighborhood grocery. We'd been prepared to drive all the way to Whole Foods but luck was on our side. We spotted his mom's BMW parked right out front, in the space closest to the big automatic doors.

"Pole position. This will be inconspicuous," Spencer said wryly.

He parked the Land Cruiser around the corner and we sauntered over to his mom's car, trying to act casual. Spencer pressed the unlock button on the remote and the car answered with an expensively muffled *snick*. We looked down at the trunk and hesitated.

"It's my fault," I told him, "and I'm used to rotting things."

Spencer seemed to consider that, then gave a brisk nod. "I'll go inside and stall my mom."

I waited for him to disappear through the automatic doors, took a deep breath, and pressed the rubber pad that opened the trunk.

I had told Spencer the truth: I was used to rotting things—as used to rotting things as any human with functioning olfactory glands could get, anyway. But this was bad. Real bad. Gagging, I scooped the whole mess into a second garbage bag, secured the top with a twist tie, and liberally sprayed the interior of the trunk with lavender Defunkify. I sniffed and sprayed again. Sniffed some more. Hmmm. In my expert opinion, the trunk needed a good airing—from a jet engine—but that would have to wait. I slammed it shut and ran around the back of the store to pitch the fish in the dumpster.

The store had provided a large caddy of disinfectant wipes by the shopping carts and I compulsively scrubbed my hands a few times while I waited. Spencer and his mom emerged after several minutes, Spencer carrying a reusable shopping tote while his mom complained, "Honestly, Spencer, I think by now I know what flavor you like."

"Debatable," Spencer said, his eyes scanning the dark parking lot. He caught sight of me and visibly relaxed. "Last time you bought the kind with nuts in it." He opened the car door for his mom and covertly motioned for me to wait. "Nuts are disgusting, Mom."

"You're so weird," Mrs. Salazar told him, sliding behind the wheel.

Spencer gently shut her door then pinned me with a look. He seemed like he wanted to talk. I had a pretty good idea of what he might want to say and it was not a conversation I felt like having at that moment. My jeans were splattered with a substance so noxious I half expected it to burn through the fabric, and the smell, oh my god. I was concerned it might be permanently imbedded in the lining of my nostrils. I also felt like I might throw up.

There were four cars and a line of shopping carts between us. We were less than a mile from home and I had darkness on my side. I gave Spencer a little wave and took off running.

I decided to visit my mom and Grant that evening. Then I decided to spend the night. Cowardly, I knew, but I could live with that. The next day, though, I found Spencer harder to avoid. Now that I was on the lookout for him, he seemed to be everywhere.

"When did Spencer Salazar transfer into this class?" I asked, strategically slipping into my desk seconds before the late bell.

Abby, the girl in the neighboring desk, gave me a funny look. "Spencer's been in Spanish with us since ninth grade."

"Huh," I said.

Despite my craven behavior and the fleas and the dead fish thing, every time I laid eyes on him (which, like I said, happened with bewildering frequency) Spencer was busy scribbling away on a legal pad. This kept him pretty distracted and I successfully avoided contact all morning.

At lunchtime I walked to La Tapatia with Madison. We bought quesadillas off the student discount menu and ate them as we walked back to school, which left me with some time to kill before Virtual Enterprise. I couldn't think of anything else to do so I went in search of Leah, who I found eating alone at a Mac station in the yearbook room. She did not react well to the news that I hadn't turned up any yearbook supplements in the Lofaros' rental.

"Maybe he didn't take them," I suggested.

She growled in frustration. "No. I know he took them. You've got to get them back."

"*I've* got to get them back?"

"Yeah. You're the one who needs to pad your college applications," she said with asperity. "Or have you come up with a better option? I hear the *Left Behind* book club is down to one person." She snatched a baby carrot out of her lunch container and chomped viciously.

"Right," I said shortly. "Well, you're the hard-hitting journalist. Why don't you tell me where to look, Nellie Bly?"

Leah huffed in annoyance and fished a stray bit of carrot out of her keyboard. "Fine. I'll think about it and let you know."

"Goody," I muttered.

I then marched off to Virtual Enterprise, where my luck ran out.

After attendance-taking, the whole class adjourned to the media center to brainstorm ideas for our group projects. Spencer found me in the back, obviously hiding by a shelf of dusty issues of *Consumer Reports*. I saw him coming and held up my hands. "I know, I know. I already called Castro's Detailing. If you'll borrow the car and drive it down there, I'll pay for them to shampoo the trunk."

Spencer prowled over and perched on the edge of the low shelf. He crossed his arms and gave me an expectant look.

"And I'm sorry I put a dead carp in your mom's trunk."

The corners of his mouth twitched and we regarded each other for a long moment.

"Anything else?" he asked.

I bit my lip. "I already apologized for the fleas."

"Fleas and dead fish," he murmured to himself. "I must be crazy."

"Huh?"

He shook his head dismissively. "I'm not mad about the fleas."

"Well, also," I thought hard, "thanks for risking your family's wrath and writing a research paper," I couldn't resist hinting, "*quickly.*"

"Hey, Spencer," a guy from Spencer's group called out, "you gonna help or what?"

Spencer sighed and slid off the shelf. "I'll see you later," he said and quirked an eyebrow. "You owe me a swim."

My first appointment after school was yet another follow-up at the rat-infested guest cottage in Montecito. Any time a technician set traps, our system automatically scheduled a return appointment for us to check them. I'd hoped this could be done by the fumigation guys when they went out to tent the place but, alas, no such luck.

I passed four patrol cars as I steered the van along East Valley Road. The rash of estate robberies had intensified and Santa Barbara County Sheriff's Deputies were out in force. The crimes now dominated local news reports, and the *Santa Barbara News-Journal* had dubbed the culprits "The Estate Bandits." Not very original but it caught on and, in addition to its galvanizing effect on local law enforcement, the name had ratcheted concern over the crimes to a hysterical level among owners of walled Montecito estates. Alarms were armed, guard dogs ran loose, and one of our techs, a guy named Gerry, reported being stopped and questioned by deputies while servicing an address off one of Montecito's quiet, hedge-lined lanes.

With this incident fresh in my mind, I waved at the guys in the patrol cars and made a point of properly using my turn signal as I turned into the rat estate's Belgian stone-paved drive. I parked in the service lot, grabbed some fresh bait for the traps out of the back of the van, and stood waiting for Irma to arrive and escort me over to the guest cottage.

Ten minutes passed with no Irma. I dialed the office and got Autumn. "Did you confirm my appointment at the estate on Lilac?" I asked.

Over the line, I could hear Autumn typing. "Nope. Left a message."

"Well, there's no one here to meet me," I told her. "The house-keeper always escorts me. These people leave their valuables all over the place."

"You're just checking traps, right? They'll never even know you were there. Don't steal anything." Click.

I sighed and started down the path to the guest cottage.

Accessing the cottage wasn't an issue. The door hardware was a terribly quaint iron latch, some kind of reclaimed antique from the looks of it. It didn't lock—it barely even kept the door closed. I knocked loudly, waited a cautious interval, and let myself in.

The place, as usual, was completely littered with expensive crap. I had to step over three designer handbags and some Prada shoeboxes in order to retrieve the attic hook. Honestly, it was starting to look like an indoor sidewalk sale in here; there was almost nowhere left to walk. Personally, if I were rooming with a giant mischief of furry plague-bringers, I would make more of an effort to keep my escape route picked up. But that's just me.

I once again scaled the sofa, hooked the ring pull on the hatch, and heaved. Then I waited for the skittering sounds to quiet before scaling the telescoping stairs. Pulling my phone from my pocket, I used the flashlight function to check the snap traps. Empty. I exhaled in relief. My strategy had worked. Rats are thigmophilic, which means they like to have their backs to a wall. They don't see very well, and they don't like wide open spaces. The middle of an attic is not the place to leave traps if you really want to catch rats.

I did *not* really want to catch rats and I didn't see any point in reducing this cast of thousands by three. Still, I felt a twinge of professional guilt. Someone was paying us good money for rat . . . well, not eradication—harassment? I decided I'd move the traps into a corner, where they might actually catch something once the rats got used to the new location. Maybe. And I'd stop by the office later to insist we come out the next time with a tent or not at all.

I panned my phone revealing the landscape beyond the attic hatch: bare plywood and vast quantities of scattered rat poop. Then I looked down at my shoes, a brand-new pair of Sk8-Hi Slims, bought for seventy dollars plus tax the week before school had started. This really called for work boots. I'd have to schlep all the way back to the van to make the switch, but that was better than ruining my nice new kicks. It would take ten minutes. Then I could get on with the important business of pointlessly annoying rats.

Stalling, I turned off the flashlight and checked my notifications. My mom had called twice and sent six texts. I pulled up the texts, which alternately demanded I answer the phone and demanded I come to dinner again. There also was a text from my dad informing me we were going to Autumn's for dinner that night, and one from Leah that read ominously, "Got something."

I had skipped out on dinner at Autumn's last week and had since eaten at my mom's twice, so there was no way I was getting out of it again. My dad insists his relationship get "equal time," thus, if I have nut loaf once a week with Grant and my mom then, by god, I have to eat sloppy joes once a week at Autumn's. Whether any of us actually enjoy these gatherings is irrelevant. Post-divorce family life is about fairness, not happiness.

I texted "Fine" to my dad, "Can't" to my mom, and decided to ignore Leah entirely. That worked so well, I took the same approach to the follow-up texts my mom immediately began sending, switching apps to check the rest of my afternoon schedule. Seeing a familiar address, I read through Autumn's notes which were, as usual, cryptically uninformative. Then, unable to come up with any more reasons to delay, I descended the attic stairs and headed for the cottage door. It swung open as I reached for it, scaring the crap out of me.

An affluent-looking couple stood in the doorway, both dressed wine-country casual in designer jeans, slouchy, earth-tone sweaters, and expensive-looking boots. The Guests returneth. Based on the large, framed canvas the man carried in his arms, I deduced they had finished drinking their way through wine country and moved on to art galleries. Both looked shocked to see me.

"Who are you?" the man demanded.

"I'm Hallie with Mayhew Pest Control. I'm here about the rats." I gestured to the drop-down stairs behind me.

"You look like a kid," the woman said suspiciously.

I get that a lot and I never know quite how to answer. I mean, I am a kid. So what? It isn't like you need a doctorate to haul away dead rats. (Theoretically, you do need a field representative license for that. I myself don't quite have one yet, because of the age thing. But my dad is firmly in favor of child labor and firmly against government regulation of small business, so here I am.) I settled for tapping the spot on my polo where "Hal" was embroidered in flowing script above the MPC logo.

"I was just about to re-set the traps," I explained, "but I can reschedule if this isn't a convenient time."

"This isn't a convenient time," the woman said coldly. "You shouldn't be in here. The housekeeper said you'd be able to treat them from outside."

"Uhh, no," I replied, baffled. "They're living in the attic and that's," I pointed to the hatch, "the only access to the attic. Actually, I already told Irma, the only effective way to approach this kind of infestation is to fumigate. If you'd be willing to relocate for seventy-two hours we could solve—"

"Forget about the rats," the man ordered, glaring at his wife or girlfriend or whatever. "We won't be here much longer; we can live with the noise."

Good. Maybe we could fumigate once they were gone. Or not. I really didn't care at this point. "Okay, well, I'll just put the stairs back—"

"We'll take care of it," the man interrupted, holding the door open with the clear expectation that I would walk through it immediately.

So I did. "Have a nice—"

Slam.

I shook my head. I was so done with this place.

My next appointment was a familiar address: a neat California ranch-style house about three blocks from mine.

"Hal, I'm so glad they sent you!" Brooke Atkinson came running down the front walk as soon as she saw me pull up. Elliot and Luca, aged eight and four, respectively, waved to me enthusiastically from the large bay window. I waved back, happy to see them. I not only exterminate tiny creatures—I babysit them!

"What's up?" I asked Brooke, searching through the pile of stuff on the passenger seat for my phone. Coming up empty, I tried to remember what Autumn had written in the notes. "You had someone come out and set some traps or something?"

Brooke scowled. "No, Mike thought he could do it himself." She motioned for me to follow and led me around the side of the house. "We've got gophers tearing up the back lawn. And we just had new turf installed! But the kids thought they were fuzzy and cute, so Mike went to Home Depot and bought one of those Havahart traps. And now we've got *this*." She flung her arm out in the universal gesture for "can-you-believe-this-crap?" My gaze followed the trajectory to a metal trap on the far side of the yard.

My neighborhood, known to locals as "the Mesa," is an interesting ecosystem. Despite its long stretch of beach and generous parklands, the Mesa's dense human population has a limiting effect on wildlife. In other parts of town you might see coyotes, bobcats, even the occasional mountain lion. The Mesa has to settle for gophers, seagulls the size of German shepherds, and, of course, our neighborhood's apex predator: the skunk.

"Oh. That's a skunk," I said, in a brilliant display of professional expertise.

"Uh-huh," Brooke agreed.

"Did you call Animal Control?" I asked.

"They said they don't do skunks."

Damn them.

"Maybe you could take it to the park for me and let it go?" Brooke suggested.

I stared helplessly at the skunk as it waddled in tight little circles inside the trap. "It's illegal to relocate wild animals in California. Once you trap them, you have to euthanize them."

Brooke gave me a horrified look. "You mean *kill* it?! That's horrible, why would you kill a skunk?"

"Why would you trap a skunk?" I countered.

"Oh my god, you can't *kill* it," she exclaimed. "The boys would have nightmares forever."

"I'm not going to kill it," I told her. Most in this field grow desensitized to a certain amount of vermin death but, as I see it, the up-close-and-personal assassination of medium-sized mammals is not in my job description. "How about you just keep the kids and the dog inside until Mike gets home, then make him let it out."

"He's out of town on business," she informed me. "For the rest of the week."

Perfect. I considered calling my dad, but I knew he *would* haul it off and kill it.

"C'mon," Brooke prodded, "can't you just go over there and release it?"

"I'm really not supposed to do that," I explained. "It's not just illegal; skunks can carry rabies and stuff."

"Hal, please," Brooke begged. "I'm here by myself, and I'll never hear the end of it if I let you take it away and murder it."

I looked at the skunk. It was very fluffy and seemed surprisingly calm. I wasn't fooled. Skunks could spray up to twenty feet.

Brooke sensed victory. "Hal, you're the best. You are totally saving my butt here. I owe you big time. I'm going to make you brownies."

"I'd settle for an old blanket," I told her.

Brooke led me to the garage where she was pretty sure there was a padded furniture blanket left over from their move. She spotted it folded neatly on a shelf along the back wall and we began shifting plastic ride-on toys out of the way. As I rolled a Cozy Coupe to one side, my ears caught the distinctive sound of dog toenails on concrete.

"Is the dog out?" I asked.

Brooke listened for a moment, then cursed. "Riley! Here, Riley!" she called. "Treat!" She frantically waded back through the toy jungle, but I was closer. I leapt over a battery-powered Batman jeep and sprinted into the yard, colliding with the eager springer spaniel as he barreled toward his promised cookie.

I reached down and grabbed him by the collar. "Got him."

Brooke emerged and took over my hold on the dog. "I told

the boys to keep him inside. What were they think—" She gasped. "Luca! Luca, FREEZE!"

I spun around and spotted the back of Luca's *PAW Patrol* T-shirt as he bounced across the yard, headed straight for the skunk.

Four-year-olds are ridiculously fast. They have very short legs but, maybe due to their smaller mass, they seem less affected by gravity than full-sized people. This being the case, I must have been moving like one of those turbocharged zombies from *World War Z* because I somehow caught him before he reached the skunk. I scooped him up into my arms and took a flailing elbow to the cheekbone for my trouble.

"No!" Luca shrieked, writhing like an caterpillar on meth. "I'm gonna let him go! Don't hurt him!"

I didn't argue as my primary concern was getting out of range. The skunk stared at us with dark, interested eyes, which somewhat reassured me. At least the end with eyes in it was the one pointing our way. Luca screeched again and the skunk twitched nervously. I started to lose my grip on his legs. Sensing an opening, Luca scrunched up as tight as he could then gave a desperate heave. Even still, I'd have kept my hold had he not somehow managed to jam one bony knee into my diaphragm. I dropped the kid and fell to my knees, unable to breathe.

Luca regarded me with a wide-eyed "uh-oh" expression for a long second, then bolted for the house.

My chest was a giant knot of spasm. I couldn't even gasp. Desperate to breathe, I flopped onto my back and that—not the barking dog or the yelling, thrashing little boy, but me, lying helplessly in the grass—*that* was the last straw, as far as the skunk was concerned. His fuzzy little haunches swiveled toward me. I shut my eyes.

CHAPTER 9

I stood in the Atkinsons' front yard with Brooke's phone on speaker, explaining the situation to Autumn.

"So you'll have to cancel the rest of my appointments," I concluded through stiff lips. I was so offended by my own stench I could barely speak.

"What, all of them?" Autumn scoffed.

"I. Got. Sprayed. By. A. Skunk," I repeated.

"Fine," Autumn said, sounding massively put out. I waited for the usual hang up. Instead she stayed on the line, adding in a hesitant voice, "And, Hal?"

What? What was this? Could this be . . . sympathy? From Autumn? "Yeah?"

"Maybe you should skip dinner tonight. I'll tell your dad." *Click.*

Ah. The universe had not gone mad after all.

I motioned to Brooke that I was done with her phone and set it on the front porch so she wouldn't have to open the door to me. She gave me an apologetic wave through the front window.

I plodded down to the curb and contemplated the van. If I got into it, it would smell like skunk forever and my dad would kill me. I briefly considered sticking my head in just long enough to retrieve my phone but decided not to risk it. I locked the van and set off for my house on foot. A jogger running past me visibly recoiled. Kids playing basketball on the other side of the street turned to stare. *That's right, people, it's all me—sniff it up.*

I was almost home when a dark SUV pulled up and kept pace beside me. The window lowered and Spencer's face appeared. "Hey, Ha—ahrgh, oh my god!" The SUV jerked to a stop and the window whirred back up. I kept walking. I heard a door slam, followed by footsteps as Spencer overtook me. "What happened to you?" he asked, shifting sideways so he stood upwind.

"Skunk sprayed me," I answered shortly.

"Did it beat you up too?"

I'd avoided touching my face but the throbbing had spread from the area just over my cheekbone to encompass my entire right cheek. I should have asked Brooke for an ice pack. "No. The preschooler beat me up and the skunk finished the job."

"Tough crowd you hang out with."

"Ha ha." I continued to trudge along. My driveway was just ahead.

"I've got skunk stuff at my house," Spencer offered. "Come with me and I'll pour it over your head."

"We've got some too." At least, I hoped we did. I tried to remember if anyone had restocked our stash after Roundup's last skunk encounter.

"Our outdoor shower has hot water," Spencer said casually.

I came to a halt.

"Speaking as someone who took a freezing hose shower yesterday: I don't recommend it. Anyway," he added, "the soap will work better with warm water."

I gave Spencer a suspicious glare. He waited, unperturbed.

"I'll need some clean clothes," I said.

Ten minutes later I stood in my bra and underwear beneath a deluge of hot water, wishing that when the Salazars had installed their fancy poolside rain shower, they'd surrounded it with one of those cute, wooden privacy cubicles.

Spencer stood a few feet away mixing water, baking soda, hydrogen peroxide, and Dawn dish soap in a big bucket. "I never would have guessed the polka dots," he mused.

"You could pretend not to look," I informed him.

"You'd know I was pretending." He grinned at my expression. "What? I like the polka dots. And the lacy stuff at the edges."

I gritted my teeth. "Spencer."

He hefted the bucket, muscles bulging in his arms. "Okay, we're ready."

I stepped away from the spray and allowed Spencer to dump the frothy solution over my head in a slow stream. It smelled like the school nurse's office. When he finished, he held up a bag of frozen peas and a kitchen sponge. "Want me to scrub while you hold these on your face?"

I gave him a look that promised slow, painful death.

Spencer grinned. "Suit yourself." He handed over the peas and the sponge. "I'll mix up another batch."

After two more dousings and a lot of scrubbing, I no longer smelled like the walking embodiment of chemical warfare, but I knew from Roundup's skunk encounters that I could expect the medicinal, slightly sulphury odor to linger for a while. Spencer handed me a fluffy towel and led me into his kitchen through wide French doors. We skirted an enormous marble island and turned down a hall, passing a pantry and a laundry room.

"You can change in here." Spencer pushed open a door, revealing a white-tiled bathroom with blue octopus wallpaper. I stepped inside, snatched the stack of clothes he'd collected from my bedroom out of his arms, and slammed the door. On the other side of it, Spencer chuckled.

When I came out a few minutes later, Spencer was perched on a stool at the kitchen island. He surveyed me with interest.

My hair, which had required repeated washings with the dish soap and hydrogen peroxide solution, strongly resembled a long-haired mystery-critter whose corpse I had once fished out from behind a water heater. One side of my face was a livid pink with a deep purple spot forming over my cheekbone and it was beginning to swell. And my clothes—well, to his credit, Spencer had grabbed clothes from the pile of clean laundry on my bed rather than poking around in my dresser. Unfortunately, Spencer being Spencer, this was not nearly as much clothing as I would have picked for myself. The running shorts were so brief I reserved them for Netflix binges in the privacy of my living room. The Surf Happens hoodie was warm and soft and offered plenty of coverage, but I usually wore a t-shirt or bra beneath it—or both. I crossed my arms over my chest.

Spencer, wisely, did not comment. He got off the stool and pulled a new bag of peas from the freezer, which he tossed in my direction. I caught it and slapped it onto my cheek. Ow.

"Better?" he asked.

No. "Yes," I said. Making an effort to sound gracious, I added, "Thank you."

Spencer opened a drawer and pulled out a fresh dishtowel. He came back around the island, unfolding the towel, which was decorated with a picture of a kitchen sponge and the words "I don't want no scrub." Moving in close, he tugged the peas away from my face and tipped his chin at me. "Lemme see."

I tilted my head to give him a better view of the carnage.

He studied me while wrapping the peas in the dishtowel, then raised the bag and laid it gently against the injured side of my face. His other hand came up to cup my opposite cheek.

What? "Uh," I said.

"You've had some week," he observed.

Spencer's hand was warm against my cheek. The expression on his face was even warmer. What was happening here?

"I need to go condition," I blurted.

"I can see that," he said gravely.

I leaned back slightly, pulling against his hold. He let go and handed me the peas.

Okay then! I gave a dorky little wave and started for the door.

"Hey, Hal," he called after me. I turned. "I handed in my scholarship submission."

Stunned, I opened my mouth and tried to think of something to say. Something that expressed my overwhelming amazement and gratitude. On second thought, I decided maybe I shouldn't mention the amazement lest Spencer get all snippy again. But gratitude: I had lots and lots of gratitude. "Thank you. Again. That's . . . really . . ." I took a deep breath. "It means a lot to me."

"You're welcome." His mouth quirked in a half-smile. "I enjoyed it."

"Well . . . that's good." I mean, who enjoyed writing research papers? Clearly the boy had swallowed too much salt water in his life. "But, anyway. Thanks." I stood there feeling awkward a second longer, then turned once more to leave. My mind busily processed the implications of Spencer submitting his paper before the deadline. Was there a procedure for invoking the third-party judging rule, or for notifying the foundation? I would need to talk to Dr. McLoren first thing tomorrow.

"Hal," Spencer called again.

I looked back automatically.

He gave me a wide grin. "I really do like the polka dots."

"What exactly is this stuff?" I sat in Madison's room swaddled in a faded beach towel as her sister worked fistfuls of scented sludge into my hair. The drugstore-brand products I stocked in my shower had failed to restore normalcy to my hair so I'd crossed the street and petitioned the Ms for help. Mrs. Forbes had not been pleased to find me bruised, rank, and dripping on her doorstep and had looked like she was about to close the door in my face when Montana and Madison intervened. They had dragged me upstairs, debating the merits of various therapeutic hair interventions, and now seemed to be enjoying themselves. Maybe a little too much.

"It's a French masque." Montana held up the jar for me to see. This would be the fourth product she'd applied. "It's made from prickly pear seed oil. If this doesn't help, nothing will."

Great. "It's really . . . pungent."

"Pungent is good. You're kinda stinky," Madison pointed out. "No offense."

"Seriously, there's only room for improvement here, Hal," Montana said bracingly.

I considered that as she proceeded to slap gunk onto my hair. It was true in more than one sense. After the unrelenting anxiety of the past week, my brain was just beginning to process the fact that my biggest worry was over. If Spencer had truly come through for me, the Verhaag Scholarship was in play once more. I might actually escape this place after all. I paused for a second to imagine a life three thousand miles from Santa Barbara, my parents, and the *Reticulitermes hesperus* Banks (more commonly known as the western subterranean termite). By this time next year, I could be away from all the bickering and power plays . . . I could be done with termite tents forever! I found this last thought so compelling that I blurted it to my friends.

Montana gave me a cautious look as she scraped the last of the goop from the jar. "I know your dad pays you pretty well but have you ever considered just, you know, quitting? There are other jobs."

People ask me some version of this all the time, like it's just inconceivable anyone would ever want to work in pest control. And, yeah, I guess it is an objectively gross job. But it's also the family business. My dad works in pest control, and his dad worked in pest control, and, since I grew up hanging around his shop, I know a lot of pretty great guys who love pest control. They get to see new places and meet new people every day. They possess a highly specialized skillset and make a good living. Let me be clear: I do not like this job—you could even say I hate this job—but that doesn't mean it's not a good job.

But Montana knew this, and she was coming from a place of having recently quit something that made her miserable in the face of her own parents' raging disapproval so, for once, I gave someone the real answer instead of the defensive one.

"His position is: it's the family business, and I'm his kid, so I work for him. End of discussion."

Her brows shot up. "Wow."

"What if you lived with your mom?" Madison offered.

I grimaced. "I'd rather kill bugs."

They thought this over.

"Okay, yeah. Bug girl it is, then," Montana concluded.

"Not really." Madison reached out and gave my shoulder a reassuring pat. "Practically no one calls you that anymore."

Okay, so maybe my busy schedule wasn't the only explanation for my lack of dating experience.

Montana handed the empty jar to her sister and resumed squishing. "So, as long as we're embracing your bug-killing career—"

I rolled my eyes.

"—there is a *serious* bug problem in the girls locker room."

"Oh my god, yes," Madison agreed.

"These tiny little bugs come out of nowhere and die all over the showers. The custodian says they've been cleaning twice a day and they can't keep up with them. It's *revolting.* We'd totally drop the class except we need the PE credit. Can you come spray or something?"

"The school district has a couple of pest control guys on staff," I informed them. "Has anyone called them about it?"

"It does?"

I nodded.

"Perfect! I'm gonna email Coach Bell about it right now." Madison pulled out her phone and began tapping furiously.

"Okay, we've done all we can here," Montana declared. "Go rinse this out and—I don't know—pray."

"Haha. She's totally kidding." Madison pinned her sister with a wide-eyed look. "I'm sure you'll be good as new."

Montana responded with an exaggerated wince.

"Wonderful," I said.

I retreated to my house so I could shower and come to terms with the results in my own bathroom. Dripping wet, my hair still felt dry to the touch. Half my face was swollen and tender. And, yep, no doubt about it, I still smelled slightly skunky. Awesome.

Scholarship, I reminded myself. The bruises and the smell would fade—I didn't care to speculate about the hair—and soon I would relocate to one of the East Coast's urban centers and never look at a skunk again. Comforted by these musings, I pulled on sweatpants and a T-shirt and walked back to the Atkinsons' house to retrieve the van. And my phone.

But my phone was nowhere to be found. (The van, sadly, was right where I'd left it.) Frustrated, I drove back to the shop so I could unload my tanks and conduct a more thorough search. I checked under the seats and in all the bins. I emptied out my backpack and the glove compartment. No phone. I borrowed a high-powered flashlight from the garage and looked through everything again. Still no phone.

I plopped down onto the running board and tried to think. Oh, god, I hoped I hadn't dropped it at Brooke's. There was a high probability that skunk was still moseying around in her backyard somewhere and he and I had bonded enough for one day. Realistically, though, where else could it be? There was an easy way to find out.

I went inside and used Autumn's computer to sign on to the iCloud website. I activated the "Find iPhone" bull's-eye and waited for the map of Santa Barbara to load. A green dot appeared at my address and I moved the cursor over it, relieved. The identifier appeared. It was my dad's iPad. My eyes scanned the display for a second dot and found it to the right of the screen. Waaaay to the right. Oh, no. Oh, that was so much worse than Brooke's yard.

I stared at the dot planted smack dab in the middle of Montecito and a scene popped into my mind: Me, earlier in the day, setting my phone down in a box of rat-baiting supplies before heading down the attic stairs to change my shoes. And then The Guests had returned and . . . aaaaaaargh.

I'd left it there. In the attic. The attic full of rats.

CHAPTER 10

The next morning I found my dad at his desk enjoying a cup of hot coffee, a muffin, and a magazine. It was a cozy setup that should have put him in a relaxed and reasonable mood.

"Hallie, that phone is company property. How could you go and lose it?"

I gave the cover of his magazine a suspicious glance. Just my luck: the latest issue of *Reason*.

"I didn't lose it. I know exactly where it is. I just have to arrange a time to pick it up."

"Okay, that's nice. And, in the meantime, how are you going to do your job without a phone?"

That was an excellent question, one that concerned me, as well. Autumn had farmed my morning jobs out to a couple of the other technicians. Between that and the hours I'd missed due to the skunk encounter, my weekly paycheck was going to seriously suffer. The evening before, after a call to Irma from the office phone had gone straight to her voicemail, I'd driven all the way back out to Montecito, only to find the driveway gate closed for the night. No one had responded to the buzzer. I'd called Irma again this morning, leaving the office number for callback, and now I was stuck spending quality time with my dad while I waited for a response.

"Maybe Autumn can print out my schedule for me," I suggested.

Seated at her desk in the outer office, Autumn leaned sideways into my line of sight and gave me a dark look.

"Do you know what a new iPhone costs?" my dad challenged.

I had already checked; replacing it was not an attractive option.

He continued, "This isn't like you, Hal. This is careless. This is the kind of thing I'd expect of your mother."

"It wasn't my fault," I protested. "The people came home early and threw me out before I could pack up my stuff."

My dad looked unconvinced. "If you don't get that phone back, I'm taking it out of your paycheck."

I took a deep, cleansing breath (conscious breathing had been a favorite technique of our family therapist) and imagined Georgetown University in the fall. There would be big, East-Coasty trees with yellow and orange leaves the size of dinner plates; stately brick buildings; and air so dry it would make my nose tingle. At least, that's how I imagined it based on the photos in the application brochure and repeated viewings of *St. Elmo's Fire*. "Sure, of course," I replied evenly. I grabbed the printout of my schedule from Autumn and retreated.

"And put an ice pack on your face!" he called after me.

My dad really isn't a bad guy. Oh, sure, he can be a hardass (especially when he's been reading his Libertarian propaganda) but he's a dedicated and fair boss. He always makes time for me if I ask him to, and his exaggerated devotion to personal responsibility means he mostly stays out of my business.

That doesn't mean I have any desire to live with him for four extra years, however. I drove to school, parked, and set an immediate, urgent course for Dr. McLoren's office.

I didn't make it. Leah intercepted me as I walked in from the parking lot.

"Hallie!" She called as she jogged up from behind. "Why aren't you answering my— whoa. What happened to your face?"

"Work accident."

"Oookay, well." Her eyes remained glued to my bruised cheek. "I've got another address for you to search."

I did a quick check of the parking lot to see if anyone had overheard. They hadn't. School wouldn't start for nearly an hour. "Actually—"

"It's this place in the Funk Zone. You'll have to wait until tonight but I'll come with you this time."

"No." I resumed walking.

"Oh, come on." She reached out and grabbed my arm, tugging me to a stop. "You're gonna need me. It's a big building, lots of square footage to cover. I'll help you look, or I could stand watch—"

"No, I mean, I'm not searching any more houses. Or buildings. Structures of any kind."

Leah rolled her eyes. "Ugh, not this again."

"I'm out."

"Do you want to be on yearbook or not?" she demanded.

"Not."

Leah glared and stepped in close. Really close. I could smell the orange juice on her breath. I gave her shoulder a little nudge. "Personal space."

"Listen up, bug girl," she growled. "I could have been on newspaper. I could have had my own column. But I wanted to be an editor. I spent three years propping up talentless hacks like Seraphina to get here. This is *my* yearbook. And if you think I'm going down on the credits page as Tyler's layout drudge, you've been huffing bug spray for way too long."

"You don't even know for sure he took them," I attempted to reason.

She exploded in a little fit, waving her hands around and hopping like she'd stepped on a bee barefoot. I took a cautious step back.

"He totally took them!" she spat.

I spread my hands. "Maybe. But I'm done."

I turned and resumed walking toward the administration building.

"You are *not* done, Hallie Mayhew!" she yelled after me.

Oh, yes, I was.

"Good morning, Hal. Fancy seeing you this early— oh, my." Dr. McLoren's eyes widened.

"Picked a fight with the wrong four-year-old," I explained before he could ask.

He hummed in sympathy. "Vicious creatures. Well. I gather you're here about the Verhaag submissions?"

I nodded.

"Coffee?" he offered.

"Yes, thank you," I said politely, trying not to look too excited. Mornings were a busy time for me. My first shot at sustenance usually didn't come until lunch.

Dr. McLoren poured steaming coffee into a ceramic mug, which he set in front of me along with some packets of sugar and powdered creamer. I tilted the mug and examined the art on the side. A skull with a scroll clutched in its teeth decorated an arcane-looking seal, under which a banner read "Society of Renegade Counselors."

"New mug?" I asked.

He gave a pleased smile and cupped his hands around his own mug, which read "You really do need help." He used that one a lot; it seemed to be his favorite. His smile faded. "If you're here to inquire as to whether I received a submission from Miss Verhaag, I'm afraid the answer is yes."

I nodded unenthusiastically. "I figured. I'm actually here to check on Spencer's."

Dr. McLoren's bushy eyebrows shot up. "Mr. Salazar? Yes, indeed, I just finished reviewing his, ah, submission."

The suspense was making my hands shake. I set my mug carefully on the desk and braced myself. "Does it qualify?"

He nodded slowly. "I believe it does."

The next time I saw Spencer, I was going to give him a hug. Okay, maybe not a hug. A sandwich. A healthy one, because that kid ate entirely too much junk food.

Dr. McLoren held up a familiar sheaf of papers. "I was just going over the rules to confirm. As entries go, it's a bit . . . unorthodox . . . but it does appear to meet all the requirements for submission."

I didn't care if Spencer had written that paper in finger paint: he'd done it, he'd done it in time, and he'd done it well enough to count. I sighed, feeling the last of my anxiety dissolve like the aspartame in my coffee. I lifted my mug and took a slow sip, savoring the breakfast-y taste despite the thin coating of fake fat it left on my tongue.

Dr. McLoren tilted his head and gave me a curious look. "This is good news?"

"Very." I reached for the scholarship packet. "Let me show you something."

"Well," he mused a few minutes later, "this is an interesting development. I haven't forwarded the entries yet, so that's not a problem. I'll have to inform Principal Rivera and the Verhaag Foundation Board . . . I suppose they'll take care of notifying the new judges. Who currently have no idea they'll be judging a high school writing contest, heh heh. Poor bastards."

I hadn't considered that. "Do you think the change will affect the timeline for results?"

The Verhaag Foundation always held their award ceremony right after Homecoming, taking advantage of the lull in the local news cycle. No one knew how they managed it, given the daunting number of submissions they received in an average (non-nepotic) year. One popular theory was that they only read the first page of each paper submitted. Another held that they simply selected the paper with the highest word count. I'm not saying I believed any of this, but I'd put a lot of effort into crafting an extremely dynamic first page and my paper was . . . lengthy.

Dr. McLoren gave a noncommittal shrug. "Hard to say. Let me reach out to everyone involved and see if I can get some answers. Why don't you check back with me later today?"

I exited the administration building and stood outside with a big, stupid grin on my face. It had worked. I felt giddy. Or maybe that was the caffeine. Without my phone, I had no idea what time it was so I wandered for a bit until I found a wall clock, which informed me I had thirteen minutes until the first bell. Enjoying the novelty of all that extra time, I took the scenic route around the outside of the buildings. I admired a loquat bush taller than the visual arts building and followed an unfamiliar yet enticing smell to another place I seldom visited: the school lunchroom. There I was astonished to discover an entire buffet of tasty-looking things: fruit, hash browns—even pancakes. I snatched up an egg and avocado burrito and carried it to the register.

"You sell this stuff every morning?" I quizzed the cashier.

She gave me a sideways look. "What, breakfast?"

"Breakfast," I marveled, handing her some cash.

"Um—" she put her hands up in front of her. "It's okay, honey. You just take it."

All this food was here every morning? I tried to imagine what it would be like to have a morning routine that involved eating an actual meal instead of exterminating intrusive varmints. This was the heady stuff my dreams were made of, folks.

Apart from the breakfast burrito, my morning passed uneventfully. I went to class, I took notes, all the usual stuff. I couldn't even remember a time when I'd felt this relaxed. I guess I hadn't truly realized how stressed out I'd been by this scholarship situation until everything was suddenly back on track. At lunch Montana and I walked to The Shop and discussed nothing and everything. She, too, was in a great mood, as she'd been fully embraced by the sailing team, and Coach Bell's continued hookup with Ms. Grijalva was making life good for his regular PE classes. He'd substituted a segment on badminton for the distance running portion of the syllabus and he'd agreed to call in the district's pest control team about the locker room bug problem.

The sun was shining, the fries were crispy, and life was good.

I bought an extra cookie for Dr. McLoren and moseyed back to the guidance offices to see how his calls had gone. I breezed through the doorway glowing with goodwill and sunscreen. I took one look at his expression and felt my glow turn to gloom.

"Hal," he said, "I'm afraid I've got to ruin your day."

"What happened now?" Montana asked, as we broke into our project groups in Virtual Enterprise.

I blew out a frustrated breath. "It's the freaking yacht club."

It took her mere seconds to make the connection, which just showed she'd been paying infinitely closer attention to all this than had my own mother. "Oh, right. One of the judges is supposed to be commodore of Santa Barbara Yacht Club, right?"

I nodded. "The outgoing commodore is Gavin Cornett." Montana motioned with her hand for me to get to the punchline already. "He's Violet Cornett's grandfather. And Violet has applied for the Verhaag Scholarship."

Violet was a serious student and, worse, she could write. The previous spring, I'd helped her find a couple of sources for her paper and even read one of her early drafts, so I could state with confidence her paper was not in the same league as mine. But it was a strong paper and if someone on the panel of judges—her grandfather, for instance—lobbied on her behalf, he could conceivably sway things in her direction.

"Okay," Montana said briskly, "so when does he outgo?"

"That's the problem. He's mid-term. *But* he's moving to Florida." Commodore Cornett, having grown tired of California's high income tax rate, had just closed on a golf course–view home in Jupiter. Or so the club's business manager had confided to Dr. McLoren. "No one knows when he'll finish loading up the U-Haul, though. As soon as he's gone, the vice commodore— who is not related to any graduating Santa Barbara seniors, we checked—takes over. When Cornett finds out about the scholarship, though . . ." I didn't bother to finish. He would stay. Of course he would stay.

"Hmm," said Montana.

"I mean, maybe he won't wait. Or maybe he'll recuse himself."

Montana just looked at me.

"Yeah," I acknowledged. "I better go talk to Leah."

To her credit, Leah didn't gloat. To her discredit, her hatred for Tyler had clearly broken her brain.

"You're out of your tree," I told her.

Leah had done some impressively dogged investigative work, searching the incorporation agreements of locally registered partnerships and LLCs and cross-referencing those with the county's Property Tax Database. Through these efforts, she'd discovered a commercial property in the Funk Zone owned by a company whose principal of record was Tyler's older brother, Wyatt—the groom from the spider-murdering mini golf bachelor party.

"I know they're in there," she declared. "It's exactly the kind of place he'd have put them. It's huge."

"Right," I agreed, "it's huge. So, even if we got in—and we have *no way* to get into that building—we'd never find them."

"I've got a plan," she assured me.

It was a terrible plan. It was actually the worst plan I'd ever heard in my life. I told her so, but, mindful of Violet and her well-placed grandpa poised to steal my scholarship, I also told her I'd think about it.

My after-school appointments were business as usual, apart from a customer in Toro Canyon who had called the office to cancel. Without my phone, I had no way of receiving change notices from Autumn so I wasted thirty minutes driving out there for nothing. Without my phone, I had no way of receiving messages from anyone else, either, so despite the extra driving and the new concerns on my horizon, it was a peaceful afternoon. At five I finished my last appointment and drove back to the office to put my gear away and see if I could persuade Autumn to print out my schedule for the next day.

She had my schedule ready, as well as a stack of messages thicker than a brick.

"Holy rollie pollie," I murmured.

I flipped through the pile of yellow slips, scanning the name scrawled in each "From" field: Mom, Mom, Mom, Leah, Mom, Mom, Mom, Madison, Mom, Mom, Mom—crap. No Irma.

"Is this all of them?" I asked.

"I'm not your personal secretary," Autumn said sourly. "I've got real work to do, you know. And I have no interest in talking to your crazy mother."

"Not an attitude that promotes successful coparenting," I chided.

"Ugh." Autumn shrugged on her Mayhew Pest Control hoodie. "And, by the way, your father says you're eating dinner at my house tonight."

"What? It's Wednesday," I protested. "Nite Moves is tonight." The season was almost over. Just a few precious Speedo guy sightings remained.

"No arguments," my dad called from inside his office. "Tonight we're having a nice family dinner."

Autumn spared me a nasty smile. "He's making chili."

As she knows perfectly well, I hate chili. The only food I hate more than chili is cucumber salad, which is the last thing my mom made for dinner before she packed her stuff and moved out of our house. Chili, coincidentally—or not—is the first thing my dad made for dinner after my mom packed her stuff and moved out of our house. Probably because chili is the only dish my dad cooks that could possibly be construed as a nutritionally complete meal. He's more of a meat-on-grill kind of guy.

We'd eaten a lot of chili that year.

I've told him many times I don't like the stuff but he forgets, or thinks I'm exaggerating, I don't know. For whatever reason, that first year without Mom hard-wired an association in his brain between chili-cooking and attentive parenting, and nothing I say or do will break the connection.

The indication that he thought I was currently in need of attentive parenting was even more ominous than the menu, and it was with great reluctance I followed his truck through town to Autumn's condo.

Autumn has a one bedroom condo on the Riviera with killer views of the harbor and a decor supplied entirely by Pier 1. I sat at her mirrored mosaic dining table and harvested black beans from a fleur-de-lis ceramic bowl filled with terrible chili. Once I collected enough for a decent spoonful, I slathered them in sour cream and sprinkled them liberally with shredded cheddar.

My dad cleared his throat. "Now, pickle, I know you have a lot on your plate." He glanced down at my not-figurative plate and frowned but continued, "And you usually have everything under control, so I stay out of your hair. But lately I don't see you functioning at a hundred percent."

I shoved the spoon in my mouth and did some fast chewing, keeping my tongue out of the way as much as possible. I still got an aftertaste of under-seasoned ground beef. Yech.

"And I'm not just talking about your lost phone, which, I assume, is a situation you're working on."

I used my spoon to corral a herd of mushy red pepper strips, the kind that came from a bag in the freezer aisle labeled "pepper and onion mix." I stacked the herd, creating a little dam to hold back the beef sludge, and searched for more beans.

"You've been skipping out on family time. Your truck got vandalized."

My head snapped up in outrage. "What? That is not my fault."

"It's because of that seedy job you took. That was a poor choice," he pronounced, then continued his list of grievances. "You skipped out on work yesterday afternoon. Your face looks like you lost a bar fight. And your Dean of Students called me this afternoon. On the phone."

I waited expectantly. Even Autumn looked interested.

"She tells me you were tardy to school on Monday."

Autumn rolled her eyes and went to refill her glass of chablis.

"Dad. I'm always late to school. Because, you know—" I tapped the logo on my shirt—"work?"

"Well," he blustered, "I shouldn't be getting calls about it."

I spread my hands. "Should I have them call Mom?"

His expression changed to one I'd never seen on him before, eyes narrowed and brows drawn downward in skinny slashes, his mouth pursed. It kind of made him look like a potato bug. "I know what this is. It's that boy, isn't it?"

I tensed, the memory of my unauthorized visit to Tyler's house crashing to the forefront of my consciousness. "What boy?"

"That neighbor kid."

Oh. Did he mean . . . "Spencer?"

"Yes!"

I laughed. "No."

"Well," he ground out, "something has been going on with you and we need to get to the bottom of it."

Oh, something had been going on with me, had it? Something like, I dunno, holding down two jobs—one that required me to *kill* things—managing the emotional needs of two parents—one who required me to *kill* things—taking four AP classes, writing a manuscript-length research paper, pinning all my hopes and dreams on said research paper, then watching my scholarship prospects ebb and flow based on the whims of over-entitled socialites? Something like that, maybe? MAYBE?!

"There's definitely something going on with her hair," Autumn contributed from the kitchen.

I gave my dad a flat stare and announced, "Mom's pregnant."

CHAPTER 11

It was late when I got home. I grabbed a bag of baby carrots and a carton of hummus on my way through the house and proceeded to devour them while I lay in the cool, dark grass.

"Hey." Spencer's shoulders and head appeared atop the wall, silhouetted against his landscape lighting.

I grunted in response.

"I tried to call you but your phone went straight to voicemail."

I crunched away at my carrots. "You have my number?"

"Got it from Monty. I thought he wasn't supposed to have people food," he noted as I tossed a carrot to Roundup.

"Carrots are good for his teeth."

Spencer studied me. "Bad day?"

I vivisected a carrot with one ferocious chomp.

"Why don't you come over." He patted the top of the wall. "I'll make you some waffles."

I considered. It was late, but there was just something about a good waffle, crunchy and slightly caramelized on the outside, soft and slightly savory on the inside. It was the perfect food. "I love waffles," I confessed.

"Our maple syrup is Grade A," he added.

Saliva pooled in my mouth. "Belgian or regular?"

He grinned. "Both."

Oh my god. Dreams did come true.

But not for me. Not tonight anyway. I shook my head regretfully. "I have to be up super early. I've got two jobs before school." One of them was a preschool co-op with a gopher problem in their play yard. Ugh. The gopher jobs usually went to someone else. This was Autumn's way of getting back at me for all the phone messages.

"Some other time," Spencer offered.

I sighed.

He dropped down into my yard and crossed to the spot where I lay, settling next to me. "Did you get a chance to read that article I gave you?"

I thought hard. "The one about the bat poo?"

"Bird guano. Yeah, that's the one." He got comfortable, leaning back on his arms with his legs stretched out in front of him. "Those islands in the Pacific, birds sat on them for millions of years. The guano fossilized into phosphate, and when they discovered they could mine this stuff back in the nineteenth century, it was like a tropical Gold Rush."

"Mmhmm." My eyes drifted closed as I listened to Spencer describe various species of sea birds, and I awoke hours later in my bedroom, on my bed, the room dimly lit by my Strawberry Shortcake nightlight, which I hadn't turned on in years.

Laura, the nice lady at the preschool co-op, was apologetic but firm. Gophers had been popping their heads out of holes and hissing aggressively at the children. Toddlers would be playing here shortly. No traps. No poison bait. And, if you please, no more gophers.

This really wasn't my bag. I used Laura's office phone to call Nick, my dad's gopher specialist. "I've got an urgent situation on the Westside," I told him. "Can you bring the Gopher Gasser?"

Nick arrived ten minutes later with his specially outfitted truck. In the bed was a modified gas generator and two large spools, each holding three-hundred feet of narrow tubing. We attached a long, hollow probe to the end of each spool and got to work.

"And this will chase the gophers out?" Laura asked anxiously.

"Lady, this'll put twenty-thousand parts per million of carbon monoxide into these tunnels," Nick assured her. "In twenty minutes these gophers'll be worm food."

I winced and glanced hesitantly at the sweet preschool teacher.

"Good," she said.

With that, I left the gopher gassing in Nick's expert hands and headed to school slightly ahead of schedule. The second bell had barely rung when I arrived at my desk in AP American History to find a cardboard takeout box sitting atop it.

"Whose is this?" I called to the room at large. No one claimed it. I caught Elena Gomez's eye as she glanced over from across the aisle. "Is this yours?"

She shook her head. "Spencer Salazar dropped it off before the bell."

I squinted at the box and gave it a nudge. Nothing inside moved. I cautiously cracked the lid. Waffles! And not just airy, Belgian ones, but also a few of the thin kind that get really crispy and supply the perfect ratio of waffle-to-syrup. They were mostly cold but the little cup of syrup was still warm and, as promised, it was the good stuff—Grade A Dark Amber. I drizzled the waffles in sticky goodness and nommed away. Breakfast two mornings in a row. I was on a roll.

Thanks to the infusion of maple-drenched calories, I was in a mellow mood when Leah caught me between classes.

"Tonight is the night," she announced in a weird, furtive whisper. Everyone standing near us turned to see what was going on.

I grabbed her arm and towed her down the hall into a fresh pool of people. "How about you talk like a normal person?" I suggested.

She gave me a scowl. "Everything is arranged for—" she looked around shiftily "—*the thing.*" I rolled my eyes. "Meet me there at ten."

"This is a bad idea," I told her.

"You've got a better one?"

"Well, I couldn't have a worse one."

"That's what I thought. We're doing it. See you there."

I tried Irma's number four times that day from various borrowed cell phones and each call went straight to voicemail. After school, I reluctantly detoured by the office again for messages and schedule updates. The look Autumn gave me as she handed over my compendium of message slips was extra caustic. When I'd left her condo the night before, Autumn had been trying to watch *The Voice* while my dad dissolved in a primordial stew of unresolved issues beside her.

It's not that he still misses my mom or wants her back or anything like that. Autumn, unfortunately, does not have to worry for her relationship or job security. I think it's more that in the universe according to my dad, things are simple: If you work hard and do the right thing, life is supposed to reward you; if you're a flake who makes bad choices, life is supposed to kick you in the butt. My mom defies the natural order of this universe. She walked out on her family and floated aimlessly until she started her fish pond business, which is successful despite her casual approach to contracts, customer relations, and traditional working hours. She's happily remarried—to a lawyer, liberal though he may be—and now she's going to have a *baby* . . . Once upon a time, my dad wanted more kids.

I flipped through my messages. Oh, great. "Looks like I'm having dinner at Mom's," I told Autumn, meeting her seething gaze. "If Dad eats with you, make sure he takes it easy on the salt." His blood pressure had to be in stroke territory right now.

None of my messages were from Irma so, when I finished my appointments, I once again drove out to the rat estate in Montecito. This time I bypassed the service lot and drove right up to the main house. The circular drive looped under a wide porte cochere, built right onto the front of the chateau-style mansion. The architectural effect was kind of Beast's-Castle-meets-Econo-Lodge. I parked the van by the front door and gave it a few hard raps with the giant bronze knocker. Nothing. I waited and knocked again. Nobody. Maybe the owners were out having cocktails on their jet or something. Still, a place this size ought to have *somebody* around. Sheets didn't iron themselves.

But if anyone was home, a few minutes of continuous knocking established they were too busy working the linen press to answer the door. I got back in the van and headed off to my mom's for an enthralling evening of plant-based meatloaf and baby registries.

"So how's the Verhaag coup working out?" Grant asked, scooping giant globs of ice cream into wide pasta bowls. The appeal of the veggie-nut-loaf had not been enhanced by the dinner conversation, which, thanks to my mom, had revolved around the benefits of homemade versus store-bought nipple creams.

I held out my hand to stop him when the ice cream level in my bowl hit the pint mark. "Not so swell. Spencer submitted a qualifying paper so we're a go for the alternate slate of judges but there have been further complications."

He stuck a spoon in Mount Mint Chip, handed it over, and began filling a bowl for himself. Strains of new age music and the scents of lavender and geranium essential oils wafted in from the next room as my mom settled in for some prenatal meditation.

"Do you think she did all this stuff when she was pregnant with you?" Grant wondered.

I gave a snort of laughter. "She didn't know she was pregnant with me until she was four months along. Then she spent the last five months freaking out about all the jazz cabbage she'd been smoking before she knew."

He looked pained. "Why do you know these things?"

"All kinds of fun stuff comes out in family counseling." The judge had made us attend weekly sessions for a year, until the therapist had advised it was not in my best interests for us to continue.

He shook his head. "So, about your scholarship?"

I filled him in on Violet Cornett's connection to the yacht club.

Grant made a *whomp whomp* noise. "That's wack."

"Yeah," I agreed.

Grant put the lid on the ice cream and carried it to the freezer. "I'm sorry, Hal. You must be really angry."

"Angry?" I repeated, startled. "No, mostly just . . . busy. Trying to come up with a contingency plan." And, you know, anger is not a productive emotion. Had I been angry when Lulu Reynolds got her dad to buy up all the remaining candy bars for the school fundraiser so she could win the trip to Disneyland, or when my science project came in second to Robert Shoemaker's, which his mom had hired a grad student from UCSB to do for him? Was I angry that I had worked my butt off on this scholarship paper—had literally put in *years* of effort—only to lose my shot at it because everything in this town was rigged so that the same kind of people always won? Was I? Ha! Why would I be angry?

"Are you okay?" Grant asked. "You're breathing hard."

I unclenched my jaw so I could answer. "I'm good."

He patted my shoulder consolingly. "Well, you know, if you're stuck around here next year, you can always come work for me part-time. Business is booming and with the baby coming, I'll have to hire someone to help with the legwork. The ladies in the Clerk of the Court's office would love you."

Only if he was planning to let me live in his office. My dad would have a fit.

"Have you thought about what you want to study in college?"

"Dad mentioned entomology," I informed him.

Grant tried to hide his look of pity behind a spoonful of ice cream, but I saw it anyway.

The moon was high and the air still as I hopped on my bike and pointed it east, coasting along the bike lane past the mile-and-a-half stretch of cliff frontage known as Shoreline Park. Parks in the city closed at twilight and at this hour the sidewalks were pristine white ribbons, clear of all walkers, picnickers, soccer players, yogis, ukulele circles, toddlers on balance bikes, and slack-lining hippies. The playground seemed peaceful, like it was savoring the quiet before morning brought on a fresh swarm of rugrats. The grass looked dark and soft. The parking lots sat empty and the fenced cliff face where spectators gathered to critique neighborhood surfers held nothing but shadows. I hit the end of the park and the sounds of the ocean built steadily as I braked down the long, steep slope, coming off the Mesa. At the bottom, I veered into the Leadbetter Beach parking lot and merged with the bike road that ran along the sand. Santa Barbara whipped by me: Shoreline Cafe, the city college on the left, the boat park, the harbor, the community pool and the beach volleyball courts. I stopped and looked both ways by the dolphin fountain, where tourists gawking their way down State Street to the wharf tended to gawk right through the bike road. The dolphin fountain would be a really tacky place to die.

Just before the skate park, I crossed Cabrillo Boulevard and turned up Anacapa, avoiding the charming, Spanish-style uniformity and aforementioned tourists of State Street. I ducked my head as I pedaled by the Fish House (in case any of the diners on the outdoor patio knew my parents) and crossed into the Funk Zone.

The Funk Zone had been a mostly forgotten industrial area between downtown and the beach until the city redeveloped it as an urban wine trail. Breweries and wine-tasting rooms moved in amongst the surfboard shapers and marine salvage yards. Farm-to-table restaurants and hipster tiki bars had come next. In other words, it was no longer the kind of place I could count on being dark and deserted at night.

Tyler's brother's building had once been some kind of warehouse. The interior had been converted to a bunch of trendy office suites but the outside was still one-hundred percent dingy industrial warehouse. I suspected the tenants found this "authentic."

Rusty loading bays covered the side of the building by the parking area—the *empty* parking area, I noted with relief—and a painted metal door along the street served as the business entrance. I locked my bike in a conveniently placed bike rack and squeezed past a cluster of tipsy women lurching their way down the sidewalk. The building loomed in front of me.

Wishing I had my phone so I could text Leah to let me in, I walked up the four concrete steps to the warehouse door and knocked as casually as possible. This was the part of this plan— okay, one of the *many* parts of this plan—that made me nervous. Teenagers are widely presumed guilty of mischief until proven innocent. Probably because teenagers are, in fact, often up to no good. Like I was, right then. But even when I have a legitimate reason to be somewhere unusual—because I'm working, for example—I am routinely challenged by random suspicious adults convinced I'm perpetrating some kind of devious juvenile offense. This is the reason I have my name embroidered on all of my work shirts. Autumn got tired of people calling her to verify my employment status.

I thought it best not to wear a shirt with my name on it while breaking and entering, so, to hedge against the chance someone would notice me by the door and demand to know what the hell I was doing, my backpack contained a roll of scotch tape and a stack of fliers advertising for the return of my lost cat. I'd stolen a photo of a cute British Shorthair off Nextdoor and I was offering a fifty dollar reward.

After what felt like a really long time, the door opened with a click to reveal Leah, peering at me from a dark stair lobby.

"Sorry," she whispered. "I couldn't get the box open."

Yeah, that was another priceless element of this godawful

plan. Through painstaking research (she drove by and read the name off the big red sticker pasted to the front door) Leah had determined the security for this building was provided by Santa Barbara Systems, the same company that monitored my dad's office. Their M.O. was simple but effective. They showed up every evening after business hours, did a walkthrough to make sure the building was secure, and locked the door behind them. At my dad's office, they also armed the security system for the night. In a building like this one, where the tenants were largely tech startups and financial firms with odd hours, there was no nighttime alarm to contend with, but Leah had still had to find somewhere to hide during the walkthrough. All the offices would presumably be either locked or occupied, and we couldn't expect the hallways to provide a place for concealment.

Leah's super-spy solution? She'd climbed into a cardboard box with some discreet holes poked in one side and had her brother's boyfriend, who played all the JV sports, "deliver" her. She'd spent the past four hours in a Blue Apron Family Plan box by the bank of mailboxes in the stair lobby. She looked a little wobbly.

"Are you okay?" I asked.

"Yeah, but, oh my god, I gotta pee!" She sprinted for the staircase. "The coast is clear. Don't worry!" she called over her shoulder.

And yet, I worried. I followed her up the dark, metal framed staircase into a dimly lit hallway with industrial-grade carpet and a ceiling hung with ugly foam tiles. Leah walked purposefully though a door labeled RESTROOM and closed it behind her, leaving me in the hallway.

A toilet flushed, water ran, and the door jerked open. "My god, that was uncomfortable. And someone tried to steal me!

They weren't as strong as Aiden, though. Next time I'll have to use a box labeled something nobody wants. Lands' End, maybe."

"Why are you saying 'next time'?"

She grabbed my arm and yanked me into the restroom, locking the door behind us. "Okay, let's do this." She handed me a thin piece of paper printed with a fuzzy floorplan.

"What is this?" I asked.

"It's the emergency escape plan for the building. The numbered rooms are offices and the rooms filled with diagonal lines are storage spaces."

"Wow." I might have found Leah's judgment questionable but I had to admit she was thorough. "Did you find this on the City Planning website?"

"No, I got it off of the back of the bathroom door. I noticed it while I was peeing."

I sighed.

"We should start with this storage area." She poked an area on the map with her finger. "It's the closest and the biggest." She snatched the paper away and handed me her satchel. "If you stand on the sink, you should be able to reach that ceiling tile."

I squinted at her.

"What? You're taller."

I rolled my eyes, looped the satchel over one shoulder, and climbed up onto the rim of the sink. Bracing my hands on the mirror, I adjusted my stance so I had one foot on each side of the faucet and, stretching my arms above my head, used the tips of my fingers to slide one of the ceiling tiles out of the way.

Leah peered up at me. "I already switched it on. Just set it up there and point it in the direction of the door."

From the satchel I extracted a shiny, black remote control

car. A claw-like robotic arm and a fisheye baby monitor camera had been attached to the hood with multiple wraps of duct tape. I examined the car, trying to make out the trim details under all the silver tape. "Hey, is this—"

"I know, I know," she huffed impatiently. "It's all I could come up with. My brother donated most of his old toys to Goodwill. Just stick it up there."

I lifted the contraption as high as I could and nudged it onto the ledge of the opening. Then I did a slow, careful squat, eased my butt onto the edge of the sink, and hopped down onto the linoleum.

"Here." Leah handed me the parent unit for the baby monitor. The display showed a grainy emptiness. She hit a switch on her remote control handset and twin beams of miniature headlights appeared in the middle.

"How are we going to know when it's over the closet?" I asked.

Leah motioned me out into the hall and whispered, "If we're quiet, we'll be able to hear it driving over the ceiling tiles and we'll follow along underneath. Just tell me if I'm about to hit any pipes or anything."

I nodded. Leah held the remote in front of her like she meant business and slowly pressed on one of the levers.

Sound exploded through the hallway. "*KSHHHHH. SHUUUUH. KSHHHHH. SHUUUUUH.*"

Leah squeaked and I frantically smacked her hand away from the lever. We froze, barely breathing, as we listened for any sounds that might indicate we'd been heard. When none came, I wheeled on her and glared.

"It's fine. There's no one here," she said soothingly. "I'm a hundred percent sure. Ninety-nine percent sure."

"You brought a *Darth Vader car*?!" I whispered furiously.

"I forgot it did that. My bad."

"Can you turn the sound off?"

"Um, no. But, it's okay, really. There's no one here."

"You have got to be kidding me."

Leah shrugged and continued down the hall, Darth Vader breathing at about seventy decibels as he rolled along above our heads. I followed reluctantly with my eyes on the parent unit. When we reached a plain door with no sign beside it, Leah stopped and pulled a second remote from her bag. There came a faint electronic buzzing and the edge of a robot arm appeared on my view screen.

"Bring that over where I can see it," Leah directed.

She set the first two remotes on the floor and took the display from me. Using the tiny arrow buttons, she panned the camera around until she found a ceiling tile with a warped edge, then handed it back. She took up the remotes, maneuvered the car into place, and wedged the claw of the robotic arm into the gap between the metal ceiling frame and the tile. The tile popped up and Leah drove the lightweight square to the side. She panned the camera again, presenting us with a bird's-eye view of a closet. Five gallon paint buckets and a roll of industrial carpet were stacked along one wall. There was nothing else.

"Next closet," Leah announced.

We proceeded down the hall in the wake of the Sith lord, checking and clearing two more storage closets. It was late and the building was quiet but I found myself growing increasingly nervous. The soundtrack wasn't helping. But we had just one final closet to go on this level. After that, I decided, I was done. Leah could search the first floor solo. I'd had all the unchecked stupidity I could handle for one night.

"The last one's on the other side of the hall," Leah commented. She hit the side-to-side toggle on the remote and Vader took a sharp left, transiting away from In the Barrel Investments and crossing to the office across the way.

"Wait," I warned, staring at my parent unit, "there's some kind of light in front of it, coming from that office."

Leah craned her neck to see. "Probably just a vent," she said. "They must leave a light on at night."

On my screen, Vader rolled forward, approaching the light source. "Leah, stop," I ordered. "It looks like—"

Vader hit the edge of a ceiling tile and abruptly plunged into the office below.

Crash.

"Aaaaaahhhh!" A panicked scream came from within the office, hitting us in stereo through the closed office door as well as the baby monitor.

"*KSHHHHH. SHUUUUH. KSHHHHH. SHUUUUUH,*" Vader said.

"Ahhhhhhhh!" Another scream.

"Turn him *off,*" I hissed. The display in my hands showed a bunch of papers and a coffee mug. Vader had landed on top of a desk.

Leah stabbed frantically at the controls. "I can't! Something broke when it fell. What should we do?"

I grabbed her arm. "We should run."

The door to the office popped open with such force it crashed against the interior wall. I heard sheetrock crunch and a life-sized Elmo doll appeared. He stared at us with wide, freaked-out eyes as red as his hair, which was mashed flat on one side, and his wrinkled T-shirt advertised an LA area hack-a-thon. I shut my eyes. Great. Our Sith lord attacked a sleeping coder. We were so busted.

"It's the NSA!" His frenzied arms waved like spastic tentacles. "They've set a drone on me—I can hear it releasing chemtrails. We've gotta get out of here. Go, run!" He shoved Leah out of the way and took off down the hall. "Run!" He screamed again over his shoulder.

I glanced at the sign on the open office door. "Doobage.com" it read, "Curated Flash Sale Site." Why me? I dashed inside and found Vader lying wheels-up atop one of the messy desks, his ominous breathing sounding a little glitchy. I snatched him up and tossed him to Leah. "You heard the man. Let's go." I took off down the hall at the closest thing to a sprint I could manage, which was more like a spirited jog. Hey, I'm a pest control technician. I don't do much running and when I do, well . . . if you ever see me running, you should probably follow.

Leah was astute enough to follow. We hit the top of the stairs just as the terrorized programmer hit the bottom. By the time we reached the stair lobby he was out the door and gone. That seemed like a good plan. I hustled toward the door.

"But," Leah protested. I turned to see her hesitating by the bottom step. "We didn't finish. We still need to check—"

"Leah," my tone was firm, "that guy booked it out of here screaming and smelling like a dispensary. If he doesn't call the police, they'll probably pick him up anyway when they see him running down the street like his hair is on fire. Someone could be here to check it out any minute."

"I spent four hours in a box to get inside this building," she insisted stubbornly. "I'm not leaving until I check that closet."

"I'm going now," I told her. And I left.

That may sound cold but I honestly thought she'd follow me out. I mean, it works on the kids I babysit. And once that door locked behind me, I couldn't get back in to drag her out. There was nothing I could do about it. I waited in the shadows with my bike until Leah finally emerged about half an hour later. My shoulders slumped with relief and I waved her over.

"Nothing in that closet, either," she declared, "so it must be in that first floor storage area, and you have to go through the first floor office to get to that one. We just need to figure out—"

"Okay, stop. Just stop," I ordered. "You saw what was in those closets, right? Paint and toilet paper. This is not Tyler's top-secret supervillain lair, it's an office building. We searched most of it, we got caught, we have miraculously avoided arrest. It's time to quit while we're ahead."

"Well, I—"

I swung one leg over my bike. "'Night, Leah."

"Oh, okay. You're tired," she said appeasingly. "We'll talk tomorrow."

I peddled across the street in the crosswalk and turned right toward the ocean. It was dark, it was late, and the trip home was all uphill.

CHAPTER 12

F riday morning brought more silence from Irma and another box of waffles. Elena Gomez watched as I filled the grid of crispy squares with maple syrup and went to town.

"Do you have something going on with Spencer Salazar?" she asked.

"Nope."

"Then why is he bringing you waffles?"

Chewing, I advised, "The glorious gifts of neighbors are not to be cast aside."

"That's not a saying," she said.

"I'm paraphrasing."

It must have been a slow news day around SBHS because, over lunch at The Shop, Montana was also on the case. "What's happening with you and Spencer?" she asked as she dug into her burger box.

"He helped me out with the scholarship thing and I got him attacked by fleas."

"And now he's bringing you breakfast?"

I shrugged and continued folding blue cheese crumbles into my mac on crack.

"And you don't think that maybe means something?"

"It means he has extra waffles."

She rolled her eyes and sucked down some Diet Coke.

But that reminded me: I needed to follow up with Spencer about Mrs. Salazar's trunk. I reached for my phone to set a reminder . . . which reminded me I had no phone. I grabbed a pen out of my backpack and wrote myself a note on the side of my hand like a third grader.

"So," she asked, "how did it go last night with Leah?"

"Hmm. Well." I considered the matter. "We didn't get arrested."

"Oh, wow, yeah." She tilted her head and nodded. "Sounds like it went great."

"So great."

"You should stop that," she said seriously. "I don't think Commodore Cornett will be a factor. The scholarship will work out."

"Did you hear something?"

She made a vague gesture with a french fry. "Just a feeling."

"Hmm." I forked a huge bite of mac into my mouth and thought while I chewed. "Maybe I'll go check out backgammon club this afternoon. That sounds legit, right?"

Montana just raised her eyebrows.

Well, it would have to be good enough. It was one of the few clubs that met monthly and I would still miss at least an hour of work to attend today's meeting—an hour I desperately needed if I was going to have to pony up for another iPhone. According to Dr. McLoren, backgammon club was chronically undersubscribed. Maybe I could talk them into making me secretary or something.

Backgammon club met in the lunchroom, which, at this time of day, with all the lunch periods finished and the kitchen closed, smelled strongly of boiled chicken. If I was doing this, I was going to have to propose a change of venue. On the far side of the room, a small group of students, all guys, sat around a table stacked with what appeared to be thin leather briefcases. They looked like a merry bunch. Even better, they all looked like freshmen and sophomores. Perhaps I could negotiate my way to officer status in exchange for transportation to tournaments. *Hi, I'm Hallie. I have access to a van. Welcome me as your liberator.*

I started forward optimistically but, before I'd gone two steps, a bony talon snagged my elbow and spun me around. "Hey," I barked.

"What are you doing? I thought we were going to meet in the parking lot to debrief."

I gave Leah a cool look. "Okay, we'll do this quick. Last night? Was a disaster."

"Please. Nothing bad happened."

"We got caught. We could have been arrested. We could have been shot."

"Now you're just being ridiculous. This is California, not Kansas."

I looked up to the heavens and wrung my hands in appeal. Flying Spaghetti Monster, save me.

"Drah-MA-tic," Leah sang.

I took a deep breath, exhaling forcefully through my nose. "I'm gonna go over there and join these nice backgammon people now."

"Oh, come on." She grabbed my arm again.

"Stop doing that."

"We still haven't searched the downstairs storage room. All is not lost!"

"And I'm the dramatic one?"

Leah continued as if I hadn't spoken. "We've come this far. We've eliminated *every* other possibility—"

"No we haven't. Those supplements could, with the exception of the very few places we've specifically ruled out, be hidden anywhere on this entire planet. They could have been pitched into a volcano. Or dissolved in a vat of acid."

"See? Dramatic. Seriously, Hal. We've got this one last place to check. What could it hurt?"

I had a feeling it could hurt quite a lot. I looked over at the backgammon club. They wouldn't meet again for another month. This was my chance to lock in an easy extracurricular and I really couldn't afford to let it pass.

One of the backgammon kids noticed me studying them and nudged the guy next to him. "Look—*girls*. And they're staring at us."

"The tall one's totally checking me out, man."

"Hey, baby," a third called suggestively, "you wanna hold my dice?"

Oh, look, baby misogynists. How cute. I turned to Leah. "Fine. But this time I'm going by myself."

I parked the van on the street in front of the warehouse at four-fifteen, hopefully timing my arrival to coincide with that moment on Friday afternoon when people started to think about quitting for the weekend but hadn't actually left yet. I hadn't bothered to check the sign on the first floor space during my previous visit. If that office was rented by any kind of financial company I was probably too late. If it was one of the tech start-ups, I could just as easily be too early. Meh. If this didn't work out, I wasn't going to cry about it.

Since it was still normal business hours, the front door was unlocked. I strolled right in carrying my pesticide tank and surveyed the stair lobby. The mailboxes lined the wall to my right, the stairs were directly in front, and to my left was a single door. Unlike the other doors in this building, which were hollow, blue-painted slabs, the door of the first floor office was all frosted glass and brushed metal. Printed on the glass in trendy, lowercase font was one word: verity.

Aha. Well, I could work with that. I pulled the door open and walked through. Inside was the hippest office space imaginable: soaring ceilings with exposed ductwork; wide, low couches with spherical rattan side tables; glass-fronted fridges full of bottled smoothies; and a bar-height desk made from reclaimed wood and topped with an iMac. Christian rock played on the Sonos sound system and three college-aged girls, dressed differently yet identically in cuffed boyfriend jeans, heels, and drapey halter tops, lounged throughout the room. Their heads swiveled toward me in unison.

"Hi," one of them greeted warmly.

"Come on in," the one behind the desk invited. "Would you like a smoothie?"

"Are you here to see Jackson?" the third asked from her perch on the fancy couch. "He just left for the day."

The others nodded, their faces sad in tribute to Jackson's departure.

"Uh, I'm here to spray for insects?" I gave them a little wave with my spray wand.

"Oh." Their expressions of warm interest evaporated. "We don't have a bug problem," the one behind the desk informed me. "We were just about to close up for the weekend."

The girl on the couch nodded in agreement. "We have a Friday fellowship meeting at Baja Sharkeez."

"This won't take long," I assured them. "I'm doing all the offices this afternoon." When they didn't look like they were going to agree, I added in a confidential tone, "Roach infestation."

"Gross!"

"Ew!"

"Ugh. I bet it's because of those stoners upstairs. Okay, fine," the girl behind the desk said. "But hurry."

I surveyed the room. Besides the door to the lobby and the two rolling cargo doors leading to the outside loading bay—presumably retained for their cool factor—there was only one other door in the space. "Can I start with that closet over there?" I asked.

"We don't have a key to that," the desk girl told me, looking bored.

Oh, for the love of larvae. "I should definitely cover the closet. If there's anything in there like, I dunno, cardboard boxes? Those can harbor roach eggs. You don't have any way to open that door?"

"Uh uh," she said, unconcerned.

Foiled again, and now I had to make a show of spraying the place. I walked over to the nearest wall and gave my tank a few pumps.

"Wait!" cried the girl on the couch. "What's in that spray? Is it organic?"

I stared at her in wonder. "Uh. No."

As usual, my tank contained a micro-encapsulated pyrethroid called Cy-kick, our go-to pesticide for residential and light commercial use. Cy-kick is synthetic, stable, and good for killing a wide variety of pest insects. For fast knockdown, we sometimes use a concentrated pyrethrin—same chemicals as pyrethroids but extracted from actual chrysanthemums instead of made in a lab. This being California, people often request that product because it's "natural" but it's only safe for targeted application. And even that product, while certified for use on organic crops, is not organic. Not that it matters; I mean, poison's poison.

"I don't feel led to stay here for this," couch girl announced.

Desk girl shrugged. "It's almost time for our meeting. Hey," she turned to me, "can you lock the door when you leave? You just turn the button on the knob and pull it shut behind you."

Yes! "Sure," I agreed casually.

Wallets and car keys were retrieved from a cabinet by the smoothie fridge and the three scuttled out the door to the lobby. I waited until I heard the front door clang shut, did a little happy dance, and moved over to examine the closet. Yep, it was locked, alright. There was no fancy deadbolt or anything, just a basic keyed knob, but it made no difference; I was a pest control technician, not a jewel thief. There was, however, a sizable gap between the bottom of the door and the floor. I laid down with my cheek on the polished concrete and attempted to peer underneath. Nope. Nada. It was a funny angle and the closet was dark, with no likely looking light switches on my side of the door. I pushed upright and sat back on my heels, thinking hard.

My dad had a camera snake, a small fiberoptic thingamajig on a flexible cable that we used to investigate tight, dark spaces. That would do the job but, unfortunately, my dad had taken to storing the newest one in our garage at home after the last two camera snakes disappeared from the office tool locker. So that put the camera at least ten minutes away, with rush hour approaching. If I left now to get it, the building could well be locked for the weekend by the time I got back. On the other hand, if I didn't have that camera, I couldn't search the closet. And I couldn't call my accomplice for assistance because I still didn't have my freaking phone.

I moved my thought process to the couch; it was comfier than the floor. I scanned the room for inspiration and my eyes eventually landed on the iMac. Surely it was password protected. I walked over and waved the mouse around to wake it up. Yup, password screen.

I slumped face-down on the desk in defeat. Were the supplements in that closet? Maybe. Possibly. Probably not. But, damn it all, Leah was not going to let me rest until I found out for sure. The spray-for-cockroaches ruse was a one-time-use kind of thing and god only knew what kind of Inspector Gadget–worthy scheme she would cook up for getting us in here next time.

I could bail. I probably *should* bail. I should use the time to select an extracurricular—a real extracurricular. Something requiring time and effort, so preferably something that aligned with my interests. Except I didn't have any interests. I turned my head to the side so I could breathe a little better and found myself nose-to-keypad with a landline phone.

Oh.

I picked up the receiver, hesitating with my finger poised over the keypad. I didn't know Leah's number. This being the twenty-first century, the list of numbers I had committed to memory was very short. Dad—not an option . . . Mom—no . . . my house— dogs didn't answer phones . . . Valentino's—hmm, yes, but later . . . Montana—Montana! I dialed quickly.

It rang several times before Montana answered, her voice cautious. "Hello?"

"It's me," I said quickly. "I need help."

"What, still no phone?"

"I'm in that building I told you about, down in the Funk Zone, and I need something from my garage. Are you busy?"

"Give me the address," she replied instantly. One of the many reasons I loved her.

I read the address off a label on the phone and warned her I'd be hiding inside the ground floor office. "If the front door is locked when you get here, just knock hard and I'll let you in."

"Twenty minutes," she promised briskly.

Waiting was really boring without a phone to pass the time. I read a glossy brochure explaining how verity could teach me to enjoy Jesus. I pruned the leaves on their ficus. I noticed a fine layer of grit covering the floor and started their Roomba. I was contemplating helping myself to a smoothie—well, I mean, they had offered—when a distinctly male silhouette appeared on the other side of the frosted glass. I dove frantically for my pesticide tank, stumbled over the Roomba, and biffed it right in front of the doorway. Perfect.

Slightly dazed, I lifted my head off the cement and apprehensively met the eyes of the person standing just inside the door.

"Are you okay?" Spencer asked. His voice was concerned but his eyes sparkled with amusement.

I let my head drop back to the floor and sighed in relief.

Spencer strolled over to the Roomba, which was beeping in distressed tones, bent down, and pressed the Stop button. "Do you want me to kill it for you?"

"What are you doing here?" I asked.

"Montana sent me with this." He held up a black canvas bag emblazoned with the words "Rigid SeeSnake." He set the bag onto the floor, grasped my hands, and hauled me to my feet. "What are *you* doing here? Joining a hipster cult?"

"They prefer the term 'ministry'," I informed him, rubbing the fresh bruise on my hip. "I thought Montana was bringing that."

"She was going out so she asked me to." He gave me a pointed look. "You're welcome."

"Thank you," I grumped.

He inclined his head graciously. "So what are we doing with this thing? What *is* this thing?"

I set the bag down in front of the closet and explained how the camera worked as I uncoiled a few feet of cable.

"And you can't just open the door?" Spencer gave the closet door a wary look. "What are you worried is in there?"

I realized Spencer was under the impression I was here on a job. Montana knew how to keep her mouth shut.

"Mmm," I hedged. If Spencer assumed I was in here doing something legitimate, the easiest thing would be to let him keep on assuming that. Except. If I got caught now, Spencer would get caught right along with me. "Maybe you should go. Thanks again for bringing this."

"Go? What do you have in there? Is it a rabid wolverine or something?" He turned and studied me for a long moment. "Why do you look all shifty?"

"Wha—?" I scoffed. "Why do *you* look all shifty?"

His eyes narrowed. "You're still looking for those yearbooks, aren't you?" He glanced around the office. "Who owns this place?"

I put my hands on my hips. "You shouldn't be here. You need to go."

"Hal. Seriously?"

I shrugged. "This is the last place we have to search."

Spencer crossed his arms. "Why are you still doing this? I wrote an entire submission, from scratch, in less than a week. My uncle is mad at me. My aunts are mad at me. Which I wouldn't care about except they keep bothering my parents. My Aunt

Susan interrupted my parents' doubles match to tell them how mad she is at me. My Aunt Julia keeps harassing my mom at the gym. Mom hasn't been to Coral Casino in a week and my dad is talking about booking a writers retreat to the Outer Hebrides. I knew this could happen but I was okay with it because you told me if I applied for that scholarship, you *wouldn't* keep doing this."

"I'm grateful," I told him earnestly. "Really, really, grateful. But there was an unforeseen complication." I briefly explained about Violet and her grandfather. "I need yearbook too."

"You don't need yearbook. There are plenty of other clubs."

"Clubs that take real time. Which I don't have."

Spencer just looked at me.

"I've come this far," I said quietly. "I'm going finish. At the very least it will get Leah to quit stalking me."

He dropped down to the floor and sat with his back braced against one leg of the desk. "Fine. Let's do it then."

"Also," I added, switching on the camera display, "Tyler really is a dick."

CHAPTER 13

The closet contained two Segway personal transporters and an empty aquarium. No yearbook supplements. I coiled the camera, put it back in its bag, and motioned to Spencer. "We can go now."

We switched off the lights and locked up without incident.

"See?" I gloated to him, as we headed for the front door. "That went great. I'm like an ant-fighting ninja spy—"

"You!" came a cry from the top of the stairs. I instinctively turned to see if "you" meant me—a response I probably needed to work on—and recognized the programmer Leah and I had dive-bombed with our Darth Vader car the night before. He obviously recognized me too. He launched himself down the stairs at full speed while another guy, similarly dressed in jeans and a hoodie, followed more slowly.

"Stay or run," Spencer queried in an urgent whisper.

"It's okay," I assured him. I hoped it was okay.

"I know you. You were here last night." Vader's victim pointed emphatically in my direction as he barreled across the lobby. Spencer moved a little bit in front of me.

"Hey, Nate, slow down," his companion called from the landing.

"I *told* you I didn't hallucinate it. This girl saw it happen. She was in the hall with another girl when it attacked me."

Spencer turned his head and gave me a hard look. I did my best to project baffled innocence.

Vader's victim—Nate, I guess—came to a lurching stop a couple feet away and continued, "This thing, it looked just like the reddit photos of government drones, and I could *hear* it releasing chemtrails, man. You saw it, right?"

Nate's friend strolled up behind him and rolled his eyes. "Leave the kids alone, Nate. There was nothing in the office."

"No, Brett. NO. She was there, she'll tell you. I didn't hallucinate it!"

Behind Nate, Brett shook his head.

"You need to come to the police station with me and tell them what you saw." Nate made a grab for my arm. I backed up a step.

"Hey," Spencer said, his tone full of warning.

"Dude, they thought I was drunk. They gave me a CUI!"

"A what?" Spencer and I both asked at once.

"Cycling Under the Influence," Nate decoded, trembling with outrage. Or maybe just trembling. "I was running for my life. I was not drunk. You *have* to come tell them about the drone," he pleaded.

I felt a creeping sense of guilt. We had scared this guy out of his pants and, if I was following this correctly, he'd then run away and hopped onto his bike in an intoxicated state instead of—well, whatever he'd planned to do. Spend the night in his office, I supposed. Maybe if I went with him and explained—

"Dude," Brett said bracingly. "They don't care *why* you were biking around town screaming about the CIA, just that you were doing it stoned."

Spencer and I shared a look, and I turned to Nate. "I'm so sorry, I was—"

"She was not here last night," Spencer interrupted. "We've never been here before in our lives. Never seen you before, either. Sorry, man."

Oh. Spencer was not good at this.

There was an awkward pause, then Brett asked, "So, what exactly are you doing in here now?" His gaze ran over my company logo polo and my insecticide tank then shifted to Spencer, who stood holding the camera snake bag like he might throw it at someone. "I know our cheap-ass landlord didn't spring for a pest control company."

Spencer turned to me with a polite expression, indicating I was up.

"Hey, what's in that tank?" Nate asked, eyeballing my insecticide tank suspiciously.

"It's after five. Isn't the front door locked by now?" Brett was also starting to look suspicious. Spencer nudged my foot with his own.

"I lost my cat," I said in a rush.

"Your cat," Brett repeated skeptically.

I nodded sadly. "I've looked everywhere. I'm really worried. I'm putting up reward posters."

"I'm helping," Spencer said promptly.

"Where are the posters?" Brett demanded.

I shrugged off my backpack, extracted one of the posters I'd printed out the night before, and handed it over. Spencer craned his neck for a look.

Brett gave me a strange look. "Your cat's name is Parvo?"

I grabbed Spencer's hand and towed him toward the door. "Well, we've got lots of ground to cover, if you could tape that up somewhere I'd really appreciate it, bye!"

We moved as quickly as we could without obviously running away. Spencer snagged his skateboard, which he'd left propped by the front door, as we scurried by. We piled into my van and took off like this was not a drill.

"You need to stop this," Spencer commented as I took a left on Cabrillo and headed for home.

Duh. I was already planning to stop. This episode concluded my poor judgment bender. I was never doing anything like this again. Ever. "Why?"

"For starters, you're not very good at it."

I gaped incredulously. "*I'm* not very good at it?"

"You haven't found any yearbook supplements. You apparently caused that guy to have a psychotic break. And you named your cat Parvo."

Okay, I felt bad about Nate. I wondered if he'd started a GoFundMe page for legal expenses.

"I feel like you owe me another taco," Spencer announced.

"If we can drive your mom's car," I agreed. "I also owe you an upholstery cleaning."

Saturday I did three routine ant sprays and tried (again, unsuccessfully) to track down Irma the Disappearing House Manager before heading off to my shift at Caddysnack. I babysat the Atkinson kids Saturday evening, and Sunday I put some time in on my physics presentation and the Santa Barbara Promise application until Montana and Madison turned up and dragged me down to the beach. The sun was hot and the water was icy. We took turns with the foam surfboard and warmed ourselves on the boulders. I got gallons of salty water up my nose and tar on my feet and woke up Monday feeling surprisingly refreshed.

I held on to that feeling through my a.m. visit to Montecito to do an emergency treatment at the Miramar Beach Resort. (FYI, even twelve hundred dollar per night hotel rooms can get bedbugs in the rugs. Use those luggage racks, folks!) I did my thing quickly and the grateful housekeeping manager tipped me off about the complimentary coffee service at the Cabana Bar. I took a moment to enjoy the scenery as I stirred real cream into my french roast. Miramar Beach wasn't my favorite—the shore's edge was crowded with small, dank beach houses and you could hear the traffic on the 101—but Miramar's lush grounds framed a magazine-perfect view and the architects and designers had worked some kind of sorcery that cut out the traffic noise. In the morning light, the sand glowed a soft pink and the Channel Islands stood clear and gray across a blueberry ocean.

I arrived at school almost on time, not really sure how I was going to solve my lack-of-electives problem, but feeling pretty good nonetheless. I strolled into History not *expecting* waffles, but optimistic about my chances of finding them . . . and instead found Ms. Grijalva.

Record scratch.

Her eyes were red and puffy, and she was not in a good mood. "There's no eating in my class, Hal," she instructed as she filled out my tardy slip. "Put the waffles away."

I'd always known this time of grace would one day end. There's only so long an interesting, intelligent woman like Ms. Grijalva could reasonably be expected to put up with a vapid meathead. Even if he would look awesome hunting sharks from his Jet Ski. But the implications for my schedule—and income— and graduation prospects—were dire. I was seven tardies away from in-school suspension and five thousand dollars away from the estimated minimum I would need to cover living expenses throughout my first two years at Georgetown.

And I owed my dad an iPhone.

"Well, that's bad timing," Montana commented as I hiked between her and Madison to lunch.

"Seriously," I agreed. "I'll have to cut back on my morning jobs and I have no idea when I'm going to make up those hours. And I've got to replace my phone. Did you know those things cost *seven hundred dollars?*"

Montana shot me a sideways glance. "I meant bad timing for Ms. Grijalva."

"Ohhhh." Madison nodded gravely. "Yeah. Right before Homecoming. So tragic!"

I gave her a bewildered look.

"In happier times, Ms. G. and Coach Bell signed up to chaperone," Montana explained.

Ah. I'd forgotten she and Madison were on the decorating committee for the Homecoming dance. Hmm, there was some extracurricular goodness I hadn't considered. I asked hopefully, "Are you still looking for committee members?"

"Nope," Montana said firmly, "uh-uh. Your glitter glue aesthetic is terrible."

"I beg your pardon?"

"Sorry." She didn't sound sorry. "The taste-level just isn't there."

"It's glue, Montana."

Madison wasn't even listening to us. "Oh my god, I feel so bad for Ms. Grijalva." She gave her ponytail an agitated tug. "They're both supervising the drink table. It's going to be so super awkward."

Her sister considered. "I'll get someone to switch with her."

"Like who?" Madison asked, her voice distressed. "Teachers hate doing drink table."

I nudged Montana with my elbow. "Can you think of any clubs that meet before school?"

She couldn't and neither, when I stopped by his office to inquire, could Dr. McLoren. "But I did finish reading this." He passed a page printed with single-spaced type across the desk. I glanced down and recognized my Personal Statement. "You sent this in with your application to Georgetown?"

"Uh-huh."

He folded his hands on his desk and looked at me, his expression serious. "It's excellent."

For all the good it would do me. I nodded my thanks.

"I don't think you should despair just yet, Hal. The scholarship committee met last night and Principal Rivera tells me it was quite a lively discussion. If she'd felt anyone had come to that meeting with a personal agenda, I believe she would have told me."

I desperately hoped he was right about that. Because this extracurricular activity thing really wasn't working out for me. And if I couldn't work before school anymore, I definitely couldn't spare any afternoon hours for club meetings, practices, or any other kind of time-wasting group activity. I said as much to Dr. McLoren.

"Hmm," he mused contemplatively. "Let me give it some thought. I might have an idea about that."

My conversation with my dad didn't go nearly as well.

"What do you mean you 'can't.' Your school doesn't start until eight o'clock."

"Seven fifty-five. Dad, it's not possible to work a seven a.m.

job in Goleta, drive to school, park, and get all the way to my desk before the late bell. I've tried. Look, I can do the local stuff, you know, downtown or eastside . . . but I can't keep covering everything that comes up. I'll get suspended."

"I'm not paying you if you don't work."

"I know."

"If you don't take morning jobs, you'll only clock two or three hours a day."

"I *know*."

He shook his head. "If that's all you're going to be working, I don't know if it's worth having you in one of the company vehicles. I'm going to have to consider this, Hal. Do you know what it costs to insure a teenage driver?"

I assumed a solemn expression. My mom's koi business owns a minivan and a Prius so her personal vehicle, a ten-year-old Smart Car covered in a tie-dyed vinyl wrap and Bernie stickers, mostly sits in her driveway. She and Grant offered it to me when I turned sixteen and my dad, predictably, had kittens. Chances of him taking away my truck—assuming the body shop ever finished with it—were approximately zero.

"Has Johan finished with my truck yet?"

My dad gave me an aggravated look. "Do you even listen to me when I talk? The *company* truck—"

I exercised enormous effort and managed to keep my eyeballs from rolling upward.

"—will be ready for pick up in the morning. If you want to leave that van in the lot tonight, I can drop you off at Johan's on the way in tomorrow. I stopped by there this morning to check it out. He did good work. I think you're going to be very happy. And it will be a lot easier to park without that spider."

"Okay, I'll what?" I paused. "Without the spider?"

My dad, focusing on his laptop, answered absently. "The guy that made those spiders for me isn't in business anymore. It was gonna cost a fortune to replace that thing. Johan found a nice ant decal for the side."

Horror dawned. "An *ant*?"

My dad looked up with a perplexed expression. "Yes, an ant. Ants are good business."

"Dad, that was *Shelob*."

"That was a custom fiberglass sculpture. And if you liked it that much then maybe you shouldn't have gotten its head bashed in."

The injustice of this left me momentarily speechless.

"And I called you earlier to tell you all of this but it seems like you *still have no phone*."

I turned and walked out of his office.

"Get a phone!" he yelled after me.

Autumn held out message slips and a printed copy of my schedule for me as I passed. She had just opened her mouth, probably to needle me about something, when my dad's head appeared in the doorway, startling us both.

"And tell your mother," he growled, "to stop commenting on the Facebook." His head disappeared and the door slammed shut.

I shut my eyes briefly and turned to Autumn, who was already pulling up the company's Facebook page. She scrolled past an ad for termite protection and stopped on the dead gopher post. My mom was the only comment. "Pete, this is terrible and inhumane! Have you no compassion??" I waited for her to delete both the comment and the original post before storming out through the garage, where I halted briefly to try Irma's number from the phone above the work bench. No answer. Perfect. I stomped out to the stupid white van, got in, and slammed the stupid door.

My schedule had somehow rolled itself into a strangled paper tube. I smoothed it out as best I could and took inventory: an ant spray off Mission Canyon and a crawl space treatment—ugh—in Bel Air Knolls. I flipped through the messages. Mom. Mom. Mom. Mom. Madison.

I got out of the van, walked back to the garage, picked up the phone, and dialed Madison.

"Hello?" she answered, her voice wary. I wondered if she was still on the library's Most Wanted list for hoarding all the Lux novels.

"Relax, it's me. I got your message."

"Oh," she said, reverting to her normal chirp. "Yeah, your mom called me. She wants you to call her back."

"She called me too," Montana, somewhere in the background, called out.

I let my head fall against the wall with a *thunk*.

"You should really go get a new phone," Madison added.

I ended the call and dialed my mother.

"Is that you, honey?" she answered.

"Mom."

"Hallie, you sound stressed. Have you been eating red meat again?"

"No."

"I don't suppose you know what you did with that diffuser I gave you? Try dabbing a little rose and bergamot on your temples. You'll feel so renewed."

I took a deep breath. "*Mom*. What do you need?"

"Oh, you got my message? Good."

"Mess*eges*," I corrected, stressing the plural.

"Hmm? Oh, well, it's so hard to track you down these days. When are you getting a new phone?"

"Mom, I get your messages whenever I check in at the office. *All* of your messages. Please stop calling my friends."

The line went silent. I held my breath because my mom was almost never silent. This was the calm before the storm. "Hallie Arachne Mayhew," she started in a low, even tone that quickly grew louder and tremulous, "you may be four months from adulthood and you may choose to live with your father—even though I gave birth to you and breastfed you until you were two and a half—but I am still your mother. And I'm the only mother you've got!"

Landfall.

"Mom, calm down." That was the wrong thing to say.

"Your father was always telling me to calm down. I will not calm down!" she wailed, as tears bubbled in her voice. "I reach out to you time after time and I expose my soul and project all my maternal energy, and all you ever do is reject me. Do you resent me? Is that it? I've made my mistakes, Hallie, I know that, but I love you. I've always loved you! Why won't you bond with me?"

I pulled the phone away from my ear and stared at it like it was a rabid mole.

Chuy, one of the other technicians, wandered in with an empty tank and glanced at the phone receiver, from which the sounds of rending garments and gnashing teeth were clearly audible. He grinned and gave me a thumbs-up on his way out. I looked around for something pointy to jam in my eye.

The clock on the wall informed me I had ten minutes to make my first appointment. If I'd had my phone, I could have

157

let her carry on this way until she wound down but, tied as I was to the landline, that wasn't an option. And even I had enough sensitivity to know that hanging up on your hysterical, pregnant mother was not an acceptable course of action.

I gingerly lifted the phone to my ear and cut in, "Mom. *Mom.* I need to go. I'm really sorry. I'll call you later. Okay?"

Her response definitely was not "Okay." But I really did need to go. I set the phone in the cradle, very gently, and bolted for the van.

CHAPTER 14

The crawl space in Bel Air Knolls was flooded. This was bad for the homeowners and worse for the condition of my jeans, but I couldn't spray a submerged foundation so my day unexpectedly freed up half an hour early. There were so, so many things on my to-do list—including a last-ditch trip to the rat estate in Montecito, likely to be followed by a painfully expensive visit to the Apple Store—but instead I headed downtown, found street parking on Figueroa, and made my way up to Grant's cramped second-floor office.

He shared the space with a friend from law school, a criminal defense attorney who'd recently hung out his own shingle and was still establishing a client base. When I walked through the door, Grant and Mike were hanging out in the small area they used as their conference room, chuckling. By way of greeting, Grant threw me a copy of the day's *News-Journal*.

"Mike's newest client," he explained.

I scanned the headline, "Knife Brandished At Panda Express," and looked up inquiringly.

Mike held up one hand in a helpless gesture. "He stood up on a table in the middle of the restaurant, waved his plastic knife at the cashier, and started screaming stuff like, 'This Chinese food is terrible! Is this even *real* Panda?' Allegedly."

"There's video," Grant added.

"Is he going to jail?" I asked, my eyes wide.

"Nah," Mike said dismissively. "That food *is* terrible."

Grant's phone rang and he got up to answer it, motioning for me to follow. We moved into his office, a decent-sized room with a large window overlooking the parking lot and dumpsters. He pointed me toward the couch and tossed me a bottle of water from the mini fridge. I settled in and considered taking a little nap.

Grant cleared his throat. "So. Hal."

I jerked upright. I hadn't noticed him finish his phone call. Maybe I'd done more than consider that nap.

He gave me a wry smile. "Have a nice chat with your mom earlier?"

I groaned and collapsed back against the couch. "I just asked her to please stop leaving messages for me with friends and neighbors." Now that I said it out loud . . . yeah, it still sounded like a perfectly reasonable request.

"What, you don't love her anymore?"

I stretched my hands beseechingly toward the ceiling.

Grant let out a hesitant chuckle. "I wouldn't worry about it too much. She's just feeling a little fragile right now."

"Pregnancy hormones?" I asked.

He pointed a stern finger at me. "I didn't say that. I would never say that."

"Got it."

"And, you know, all this," he gestured vaguely at his own stomach, which was kind of hilarious, "is making her question what sort of mother she'll be—what sort of mother she *is*," he corrected quickly. "She's asking herself why you two aren't closer, why you don't spend more time together . . ." he trailed off, tact-fully leaving the "blah, blah, blah" unspoken.

I tried to think of a kind way to phrase "because she makes me want to surgically alter my face, assume a new identity, and move to Guam" and came up empty. I loved my mom, I did. But I could love her just as much—probably more—from the other side of the country.

Grant shrugged. "It doesn't really matter. The two of you are very different people, and this baby, he or she will also be a completely unique person. Who may not share her love of açaí bowls and Deepak Chopra. It's hard for her, but it's some-thing she'll have to come to terms with. With regard to both her children."

"Well," I said, a little helplessly, "I'm sorry."

Grant nodded. "Great. Then you can go to prenatal yoga with her."

"What?"

"It's yoga for pregnant ladies. Very soothing, she tells me. Good for mobility and maintaining muscle tone." He rubbed his forehead, looking a little green. "Pelvic floor strength."

What was . . . no. Just no. Oh my god, no. Absolutely not. I sighed in resignation. "When?"

"Thursdays at six-thirty, I think. I'll check the time and text y— leave a message for you at the shop."

"Great."

"Great!"

When I made no move to clear out, Grant raised an eyebrow. "Anything else?"

Any qualms I'd felt about asking for professional favors had dissolved at the words "prenatal yoga." I shot Grant a speculative look. "Does Mike handle CUI's?"

I dropped off the van at the shop, Ubered home, and, since the tide was low, took the dog for a stroll on the beach. The sun carpeted the water with wide swaths of yellow sparkles and the sky shone unreasonably blue. The ocean had pulled back to reveal the rows of long, narrow rock formations that hid just beneath the surf and sand. Nestled between these dragon spine formations, tide pools teemed with anemone, sea stars, and busy little shrimp. Roundup and I walked halfway to Hope Ranch before turning back. Roundup terrorized a schnauzer and ate a dead crab and we were both flagging as we hauled ourselves back up Thousand Steps to street level. I used the hose to rinse off all six of our feet then collapsed in the warm grass of my backyard. Ahhh.

The hollow *thunk* of bare feet landing on the dock box intruded on my moment. I lifted my head to watch Spencer as he strolled across the yard, shirtless, as usual. He wore a pair of knee-length jogging shorts and looked good in them. I caught myself staring and flopped back onto the grass as Spencer folded down beside me.

"I can't decide," he mused, "whether I want to know what that stuff on your jeans is or not." He studied my face. "I'm thinking not."

I bent a crawl space–besludged knee and held it up for inspection. "Pretty gross," I acknowledged. "Could be worse."

"Bad day?"

I considered. "Pretty gross. Could be worse ."

His eyes met mine. He had pretty eyes. "Did the waffles help?"

"Waffles always help."

"So I was thinking," he said, rolling over onto his stomach and propping himself up on his elbows, "we should go to Homecoming together."

"Homecoming," I repeated slowly, trying to match a definition to that word that made sense in this context.

"You know, the dance? Also a football game. But now that Montana and Madison are off the dance team, we don't have to go to those anymore."

"They want to go to the Homecoming dance?"

"No. Well, maybe. But I meant you and I should go. The two of us."

I squinted at him. "Why?"

He squinted back. "Because, although you're the busiest human I've ever met, it is customary, when in high school, to take that night off, put on fancy clothes, and go to a school-sponsored event with a handsome and debonair date."

I stared. I couldn't help it. "You want to go on a date?"

"Yes," he said, speaking clearly. "With you."

I shook my head. "No."

"Why not?"

"I . . . just . . . never do that stuff. Why do you even want to?"

Spencer, looking amused, cradled his cheek in his hand and answered, "Because I like you."

"You like me." I struggled to process that.

He raised his eyebrows a couple of times. "I *like* like you."

I was skeptical. "Since when?"

He sat up, putting a bit of space between us, and sighed. "Since, I don't know, second grade?"

I sat up, too. "What? No."

"Yes."

"This is the first I've heard of it."

"That's because you've been ignoring me since about third grade."

"I have not," I declared.

"You have. We used to be friends, remember? We hung out all the time, us and Monty and Madison. Then you just stopped playing with me."

Third grade was the year my mom left. "In third grade I started going to after-care. I wasn't ignoring you. I wasn't even home."

"You're well past your after-care days. What about lately?"

"What *about* lately?" I challenged.

"We've been at the same school since ninth grade. You haven't spoken to me in years—until you realized you needed me for something."

Stung, I retorted, "It's not like we have a lot in common to talk about."

"What's that supposed to mean?" he demanded.

"Oh, come on, Spencer. I work two jobs and my GPA is three-hundredths of a point behind Eva Laurales', and she's going to be valedictorian. You sleep through class—"

"I do not."

"Freshman English. You slept through that class every day."

"That class was boring. I'd already read every book on the syllabus."

"You don't take anything seriously. You cut class to go surfing—"

"Only when I have study hall."

"—you throw parties on school nights—"

"I have friends and, yes, they come over sometimes."

"—after which your friends barf in my yard—"

"That happened *one time*. Anders ate a bad tuna taco."

"—and you seem to be deathly allergic to shirts."

His jaw literally dropped. He recovered and glared at me. "Your crappy opinion of me didn't stop you from asking me for help when you needed something from me. And I *did* help you, because we used to be friends, and because I wanted you to notice me. I'm not proud. I thought, 'Hey, here's my chance.' So I wrote what you wanted. And I did it in two days when, apparently, it took you *years*, so maybe I'm not such a flake after all."

I took a calming breath. "I never said you were a flake. And I very much appreciate you writing that submission. I can't imagine how you managed twenty-five pages in two days."

He shrugged. "I didn't. The twenty-five-page minimum was for the research paper. I went with the poetry option."

I gaped. "You wrote a poem."

"Yes, I wrote a poem. I'm not writing a twenty-five-page homage to my extended family's bizarre delusion. I wrote the damn poem. I had fun with it."

I'll admit, I'd pretty much forgotten that was an option. No poem had been selected as the winning submission ever, so there was no point. Plus, it had to be a narrative poem, inspired by the work of Robert W. Service, and there were strict structural requirements—*x* number of lines, with a specific rhyming format. Writing something that complied with the guidelines would be a nightmare. I stared at Spencer and repeated, "*You* wrote a poem?"

His brows descended. "Yes, *I* wrote a poem. My dad is a best-selling author, you think I can't write a poem?"

That's exactly what I'd thought. "Oh, come on, Spencer, you'll have to forgive me for underestimating your scholarly devotion. You're not even going to college."

"Says who?"

I threw up my hands. "Dr. McLoren. He told me himself that you weren't competing for the Verhaag Scholarship because you're not applying to colleges."

Spencer rubbed the back of his head, looking deeply frustrated. "I want to study creative writing. I'm applying to combined B.A./M.F.A. programs. That scholarship covers undergraduate programs only. And, you know what, I was wrong: apparently I do have some pride. If this is honestly what you think of me, why don't you just go back to not speaking to me. I'm out."

"Spencer . . ." I began, trying to think of what I wanted to say. Nothing occurred to me.

He stormed across the yard without looking back and disappeared over the wall.

The next morning, I rode with my Dad to work and he drove me to the body shop when it opened. The Ranger looked naked without Shelob. And boring. I shook my head sadly.

"Don't even start," my dad warned. "I already talked to Refugio at Coastal Auto Wrap. He's going to do you a nice spider decal. You won't even notice the difference."

This assertion was so ludicrous I didn't bother responding.

"You'll get better gas mileage," he called after me, as I pulled out of the lot.

Sometimes I feel like no one in this world understands me . . . and it's because no one in the world understands me.

Ms. Grijalva was at her desk three minutes before the late bell, looking even more miserable than she had the day before. There were dark circles under her eyes and, in place of her usual insulated glass mug of freshly infused herbal tea, she clutched desperately at a steaming espresso shot from Starbucks.

There were no waffles.

Elena gave me an inquiring look from across the aisle, which I ignored.

Montana was not so easily discouraged.

"Okay, what did you do to Spencer?" she accused at lunch.

"I didn't do anything to Spencer."

"You did something. He's mad, and Spencer is never mad."

Madison stared at me with big eyes. "Not ever," she agreed.

I shrugged. "He asked me to Homecoming."

She gasped and leaned in closer.

"I said no," I added quickly, before she could start with the squeeing and the wardrobe planning.

"It would take more than that to tick off Spencer," Montana said prosaically.

"Whose side are you on?"

"Hmm." She gave me a thoughtful look. "Do we have sides now?"

I rolled my eyes. "He's just being touchy. He'll get over it."

But Wednesday I was forced to mourn the time of waffles as truly past, and the only person in AP American History who looked more tired than me was Ms. Grijalva. I wondered if she was having second thoughts about dumping Coach Bell.

I mentioned the possibility to Montana in Virtual Enterprise.

"Well, he is pretty hot," she said.

"If those two crazy kids patched things up," I reasoned, "I could probably count on Ms. G. arriving late for at least the next month." I'd be back in business. "Also, she seems really sad."

"Mhm," Montana offered noncommittally.

"She's one of the good ones; I hate to see her sad."

"Do you think you might be a little over-invested in this for some reason?" she asked pointedly.

"Yeah. I need to work."

"And you're totally not projecting any of your own unresolved feelings or experiences here, right?"

I gave her a flat look.

"Okay, just checking."

That evening, though I conspicuously hung out in my backyard after Speedo Guy ran by, Spencer did not make an appearance. I had sort of gotten used to him turning up and I was starting to have funny feelings about our last encounter. I woke in the middle of the night with my mind replaying our last conversation on relentless loop. I found this incredibly annoying because a) it was not productive and b) I really needed my sleep. I'd been waking up an hour earlier than usual in hopes of getting some extra time in at work, having all but given up on Irma. The specter of an expensive new phone purchase haunted me and I also needed to come up with the application fee for the Santa Barbara Promise program. Unfortunately the early-to-rise strategy had yet to yield any extra income. I guess there was a limit to how early in the morning people wanted their pest control technician to turn up at the door.

Thursday morning was again a bust. No one called in to the office for an emergency, pre-dawn gutter brushing. Since I definitely was *not* projecting, regardless of what Montana kept insinuating, it seemed to me I had nothing to lose by doing a quick welfare check on Ms. Grijalva. I headed to school a full hour early and made my way to her classroom to wait.

She was already there, her laptop and an oilcan of Rockstar open on the desk in front of her.

"Oh! Good morning, Hal. Do you need something?" I'd obviously interrupted her slide into caffeine addiction but she made a valiant effort to put on her Enthusiastic Educator hat.

"Just made it in early today." I eyed the energy drink. "Those things will kill you, you know."

"Oh, ha. Yeah. I just needed an extra boost this week. Is it the weekend yet?" She gave a forced chuckle.

If only. My Friday night babysitting clients had canceled due to pinkeye and the Caddysnack was rented out for a private event Saturday afternoon so, for once, I looked forward to something resembling a normal weekend. "Only about thirty interminable hours to go," I joked.

Ms. Grijalva's face crumpled. She dropped her head to the desk and let out a keening whimper.

Okay, this seemed . . . bad. Unfortunately, I had absolutely no idea what to do about it. I didn't have much practical experience conversing with people in emotional distress. I did it with my mom periodically, but those conversations were pretty one-sided and I couldn't tell you what prompted them. (If I knew, I would make sure never, ever to do it again.) My dad subscribed to the suck-it-up school of emotional actualization, and Madison and Montana had each other. This was not my bag.

But Ms. Grijalva was clearly suffering. I wracked my brain and finally fell back on the meager wisdom gained from my four years of babysitting experience. I patted her gently on the shoulder and quoted, "It's okay to feel sad sometimes."

Or so says Daniel Tiger.

The shoulder under my hand shook as she began to sob. I snatched my hand back. Oops.

After a long moment, though, Ms. G. lifted her head and

pulled a tissue from the box at the corner of her desk. She wiped her eyes with careful dabs, probably trying to preserve her makeup. It was too late for that but I refrained from saying so. She dropped the tissue into the trash, reached out, and grabbed my hand. "Thank you, Hallie. I think I needed to hear that." She looked away and said quietly, "The way you kids gossip, I'm sure you've heard about Brad—Coach Bell—and me."

After a moment's hesitation, I nodded. It always freaks me out a little when I'm reminded teachers have first names.

"I just—it's been less than a week and, and, I m-miss him so much. I never imagined he'd end it that way."

I felt my eyes go wide. Coach Bell had ended it? He was the dump*er*? I tried to envision a universe in which this made any sense. "I kind of thought, ah . . ." I searched for the right words, ones that would convey, "How in the world did a master's degree-holding champion of intersectional feminism get dumped by a man who thinks it's pronounced 'green-witch mean time'?" without giving offense.

Ms. G. seemed to know where I was headed.

"I know, Brad and me . . . it seems crazy, right? I mean, back in high school, he wouldn't even have looked at me, I was such a nerd. But now we're adults and that doesn't matter so much. Other things—completely different things—matter now, but I just *like* him. I like him so much. Oh my god, though, do you know what my sisters would say if I brought him home? He works so hard and he's a great football coach but I know what my sisters would think about that. And he's got the sweetest heart, but some of the things he says . . . I'm not sure, but it seems like he may think the Queen actually rules England?"

I nodded in confirmation.

"Well, I don't care about any of that anymore. If I could do it over, *of course* I would introduce him to my family! Maybe I'd worry a little about my sisters saying something mean, but I know he can take care of himself. I just wish he'd give me the chance to apologize."

She dropped her head into her hands. I gave her shoulder another tentative pat and hustled out to the vending island, where I bought a bottle of water. I returned to the classroom and set the bottle by her arm.

"Thank you, Hal," she said, her face still hidden. "I apologize for falling apart on you like this. Could you give me a few minutes, please?"

"Sure," I agreed hastily. I left as quietly as I could, snagging the can of Rockstar on my way out.

CHAPTER 15

When I stopped by the office after school, Autumn all but threw my job list at me and declared she was done printing out my schedules and she was never taking another message for me as long as she lived. She made this announcement in a booming, harpy voice that flushed my dad from his office, and he emerged to inform me I'd better have a phone by tomorrow morning or he was going to buy one and garnish my paycheck for the cost.

"And if it happens that way, I'm also billing you for my time while I'm at the Apple Store," he threatened.

So, after work, I stood in Montana and Madison's driveway and explained I was going to have to skip out on our plans to see a movie that evening.

"Hal." Montana gave me a severe look. "You literally haven't been to a movie with us in years."

"We could go tomorrow," I said.

She instantly vetoed. "It's crowded on Fridays."

"Why don't we just stop at the Apple Store on our way to the theater?" Madison offered.

I took a deep breath and let it out slowly. "I'm not going to the Apple Store."

This week, this month, this *existence*—all at once, I was at my limit. A normal girl in my situation would have options. She might get in a cathartic fight with her parents and distract herself from the ceaseless unfairness of life with a facial piercing or some rebellious sex. But I didn't want to fight with my parents; they inflicted plenty of drama on my life without any provocation at all. Piercings? Not safe in my line of work. And the only conceivable candidate for a rebellious sex partner had just bailed over my back fence, never to return. But no longer would I stand idly by while my family indulged their every sloppy emotion and entitled socialites toyed with my future. It was time to take charge of my destiny! Insofar as that was possible.

"I'm going to get my phone back," I said.

Montana and Madison stared at me in silence for several beats. Montana gave her head a little shake. "I'm sorry, you're going to get your phone back . . . from the attic of some random people's guest cottage in Montecito?"

"I'm sure it's empty by now." And if it wasn't, I would knock. Easy.

"All of this illicit breaking and entering you've been doing lately is seriously screwing with your good idea/bad idea barometer," Montana stated. "Let me be very clear: this is a *bad* idea."

I waved my hand. "It'll be fine."

This was happening.

"I don't get it," Madison frowned, a single wrinkle appearing on her perfect, porcelain brow. Her sister backed the Dance Mom–mobile out of their garage at about thirty miles per hour and halted at the end of the drive with a screech. "Why didn't you do this, like, a week ago? All this time you haven't had a phone."

I gave a small, wistful sigh. "Yep. All this time."

I went back across the street to my house, made some dinner, and walked the dog. Then, just in case traffic was still bad on the 101, I started my homework. I wasn't stalling, I was just . . . okay, maybe Montana was right. Maybe this was not my best idea ever.

At seven-fifteen, my dad walked in the door, having finished his weekly Happy Hour with Autumn at Chuck's Hawaiian Grill, where the free appetizer buffet closed at seven.

"Did you get a phone?" he asked immediately. "I'm not kidding. I'll bill you if I have to do it."

I shut my laptop. "I'm about to."

"They close at eight," he warned.

"I'm going now," I said, my courage restored. I judged it best not to mention *where* I was going.

Locating an address in Montecito is always tricky. It's a village of tortuous lanes lined with stately walls and towering hedges, and it's only the rare house that can actually be seen from the road. Finding the right wall can take several passes, even in daylight. I was a frequent flyer to the rat estate but, in the dark, I almost missed the gap in the appropriate hedge.

I proceeded slowly down the Belgian stone-paved drive. The grounds were dimly lit in accordance with local light pollution ordinances and I observed zero signs of life. I pulled off into the service lot and parked. The service lot was located behind a dense grove of olive trees—you don't want unsightly staff vehicles ruining your fancy view—and marked paths of varying widths led off through the trees in several directions. The narrowest of these was the footpath leading back to the guest cottage. The very occasional solar landscaping light offered weak guidance through a shadowy tunnel of claw-like branches. I cautiously picked my way across the gravel, grateful I'd have the flashlight on my phone on the return trip. This part of Montecito wasn't brimming with wildlife but rattlesnakes could turn up in the darnedest places. It was also kind of spooky.

The sconces by the guest cottage door were off and the interior was dark but I knocked out of habit. No one called out and I let myself in, hit the lights—and was instantly confronted by a space exploding with signs of habitation: rumpled bed sheets, wet towels hanging over the bathroom door, used wineglasses on the ikat ottoman. I froze in panic.

These slobs should have been gone by now! A total absence of people was the only logical explanation for Irma going dark on me. It was pretty common, after all, for estate owners to put the household staff on furlough while they were residing at one of their other properties. I had reasonably concluded the joint would be empty.

But The Guests were definitely still around and, from the looks of it, they had not been idle during their extended visit. The interior of the cottage was jammed to its artfully rustic beams with fancy crap. These people must have set the goal of buying out every store in the tri-county area. And, extremely fortunately for me, they appeared to be out working on that right now.

I shook off my panic and headed for the attic access. A quick pull and I was up the telescoping stairs where, I was relieved to see, my traps still sat empty along the walls. My phone was just where I'd left it and looked okay. The battery was long dead but it was rat poo–free. I snatched it up and scurried back down the stairs. Painfully aware that The Guests could return at any moment, I gave the stairs a hard shove, paused just long enough to make sure the hatch snapped all the way shut, and headed for the door. At the last second, I remembered the lights and hit the switch as I walked through the doorway, bracing for darkness. Instead, a blinding beam of light slapped me right in the face.

"Stop," commanded a stern voice. "Get down on the ground."

Investigator Beamish, with the Santa Barbara County Sheriff's Office, had light brown hair just starting to go gray and a suspicious mind. Probably a suspicious mind was an asset if your job title was "Investigator," but this time the mind in question suspected *I* was one of the notorious Estate Bandits, so I was not impressed. He based this assumption on a single, isolated, purely circumstantial detail: "You were apprehended exiting a cottage containing over three million dollars' worth of stolen property."

So all that stuff . . . oh.

I squirmed in a molded plastic visitor's chair by Investigator Beamish's workstation. The Sheriff's County Office had awful furniture. "I was only there to get my phone." I'd already explained this. Twice.

"Seems like a 'pest control technician' would have plenty of access to houses around here. Lots of opportunities to scope out interesting properties."

I'd have been mortally offended had I not recently been using my job for just that purpose. With that in mind, I opted to keep my mouth shut.

He switched tacks, giving me a much kinder look. "Would you like to tell me what happened to your face? That's quite a bruise."

Uh huh. Not for nothing, I've been a junior member of the ACLU since sophomore year Civics class. I follow them on Twitter.

"If you're going to question me, I'm supposed to have a parent or guardian with me," I informed him.

Inspector Beamish didn't like that much but I was still a minor so he had to let me make a call. Like most children of divorced parents, I had a well-researched understanding of which parent was the preferred one to involve in a whole catalogue of situations. Unfortunately, this particular situation was not in the catalogue. I couldn't imagine either parent being anything but a source of chaos and embarrassment at the Sheriff's Office.

In the end, I called Grant. He arrived, accompanied by Mike, and they got me released within the hour.

Inspector Beamish kept my phone.

My dad was not a happy camper. *"Breaking and entering."*

"Really just entering."

"Hal!"

I spread my arms. "You said I should get my phone back."

"I said *buy a new one.*"

"I already had a perfectly good one and I knew exactly where it was. I tried to clear it with the house manager and she never called me back. I took the initiative."

My dad roughly scrubbed his hands over his face then leaned forward and met my eyes. "Pickle, you could have been hurt. You *did* get arrested."

It was morning and we sat in his office waiting for the city impound lot to open so we could retrieve my truck. Autumn, who has a strict policy of non-involvement when it comes to the parenting of yours truly, had gone on a bagel run to Panera.

"Detained for questioning," I corrected soothingly. "And I was released without charges. Nobody got hurt. Grant says there won't even be a record." Unless, you know, they arrested me later.

My dad had gone to bed by the time Grant had dropped me off at my house the night before. I hadn't seen any point to disturbing his peaceful evening, so the first he'd heard of last night's fiasco was when I'd ambushed him by the coffee maker at 5:47 a.m. and informed him I'd need a ride to work. He was still processing.

"What do you think colleges will do if they find out about this?"

I didn't have an answer for that. I was worried. But I had a lawyer, I had work orders proving I'd been previously authorized to be in that guest cottage, and I had accurately described the exact location of all my rat traps in the attic. And, incidentally, I had never stolen anything, much less art, jewels, or twenty-eight thousand dollar Louis Vuitton reusable shopping bags. I could only hope it would be enough.

My dad crossed his arms. "You called *him*."

Ah-ha. There it was. Sure, getting stuffed into the back of a patrol car, hauled off to the Sheriff's Office, and accused of participating in a multi-million-dollar theft ring was bad, but we couldn't let it distract us from the real issue: I called my stepfather instead of my dad.

Divorce is a glorious thing.

"He's an attorney, Dad."

"I should have been there."

"Well, I have to go back this afternoon," I said brightly. "You can come with me then." He frowned and I had a sudden thought. "Hey, maybe you can get them to give my phone back."

Dad gave me a look of deep displeasure and I tactfully decided to study my Vans for a while. We sat like that until the city impound lot opened for the day, at which point he got up and left the office without a word. I picked up my backpack off the floor and followed.

"So," I asked, as I climbed into the passenger seat of his truck, "do you think you can get Autumn to print out my schedule one more time?"

It took a surprising amount of time—and money—to get a car out of the city impound lot.

"What's this charge?" I asked, pointing to a two-hundred dollar line item.

"That's for the tow," the guy in the booth explained.

"I didn't order a tow," I protested.

The guy in the booth laughed so hard he had a coughing fit. He drank some coffee and laughed some more. "You've got a funny kid," he said to my dad.

My dad, looking stoic, handed him a credit card. I was sure I looked considerably less stoic. That was probably coming out of my paycheck.

I didn't waste any time getting to school but I was forty-seconds late to American History. Ms. Grijalva gave me an apologetic look as she filled out my tardy slip and I trudged to my desk. I was starting to adjust to all this bad luck. It was my new normal.

Midmorning, I responded to a summons from Dr. McLoren and took the opportunity to fill him in on my recent troubles with the law. I thought I might need him later as a character witness.

Dr. McLoren didn't seem all that concerned. "The papers specifically said the police were looking for a white cargo van in connection with the Estate Bandit crimes. Don't you drive a truck with a giant spider on it?"

Um, yes, except for the last week or so, when I'd been driving

. . . a white cargo van. I pressed a hand to the side of my temple. I felt a headache coming on.

"Now, the reason I called you in." He reached around and pulled a sheet of paper off the top of his file cabinet. "I have official notification from the Verhaag Scholarship Judging Committee that they have received and are reviewing submissions from these students. Your name is on there, of course, along with Spencer Salazar's and Britta Verhaag's. But here's the part you will find interesting: the letter is signed by all the committee members and Commodore Cornett's name is not among them."

I held out my hand and he gave me the paper. The signature labeled "Commodore, Santa Barbara Yacht Club" read "Mitchell Putnam."

"Cornett moved to Florida?" I asked.

Dr. McLoren shrugged. "I'm not sure of the circumstances but I'm told he stepped down sooner than expected."

I collapsed back into my chair, overcome with relief. It was official: I was going to college!

As long as I didn't go to jail first.

Montana's face took on a smug expression when I gave her the news about Commodore Cornett but her response was a typically mild, "Really? How perfect."

"Everything is back on track. Except for the part where I might go to jail."

Giant eyeroll. "You didn't take anything. You'll be fine. I mean, you were hired to be there, right?"

"Mmm. Mostly. I gave Irma's number to Investigator Beamish so he can confirm. Maybe she'll call *him* back."

Montana gave me a sideways look. "So, does this mean you're done hunting yearbook supplements?"

"Oh yes," I confirmed. Now I just had to tell Leah.

I had back-to-back appointments scheduled after school, to be followed by my return visit to the Sheriff's Office, so I only had a couple of minutes to break the news to Leah. I waved at her from the door of the yearbook room and she joined me out in the hall.

"I'm out," I told her, "for real this time."

"Oh, come—"

I shook my head. "We've looked everywhere we can think of. There's nowhere else. You should probably consider those things gone forever."

"Then Tyler wins! That is unacceptable. I refuse to accept that."

I sympathized but . . . "Sorry."

"Just give me a day to do a little more research. I'm sure I can find some—"

"Ahhhhahahaha!" We both turned as Tyler strode out of the yearbook room. "Look at you two *losers*. Commiserating like the sad little hags that you are. You think I wouldn't find out what you've been up to?"

I'd recently spent quality time with a Sheriff's investigator, so I knew exactly what to do. I stared up at the ceiling tiles and hummed a jaunty tune under my breath. What was it about public school commissions that inspired architects to insert horrors like hung Styrofoam ceilings and asbestos wall tiles into otherwise lovely buildings?

"No clue what you're talking about," Leah said scornfully. "Have you been sniffing contact cement again? I'm gonna tell the student council people they need to keep their poster supplies locked up."

Tyler gave us a nasty smile and held his phone up so the display faced us. He tapped play and we watched, frozen, as my grainy likeness walked up the darkened steps of Tyler's brother's warehouse. The door opened as Leah, unseen by the camera, pushed it open, and I walked inside.

Tyler swiped forward and a second video appeared. Me again, this time in daylight, stepping out of the white van. I winced as, again, I walked up the steps to the building and went in.

He lowered his arm and moved in close. "You morons think we don't have cameras? And my mom says you've been sneaking around our house too."

I decided my best option was to brazen this out. "You mean working? Yeah, it's what I do."

"No one in that building hired you, bug girl. I asked around."

This was bad, bad, bad. I shrugged.

He pitched his voice low and ranted furiously. "I know what you're doing. You're looking for those yearbook supplements. Well, when *I* do things, they get done right and, believe me, you're never finding them."

Leah glared back at him. "Oh, we've got lots more places to look," she spat, dodging my elbow. "Give us time."

"HA!" He jumped back and pointed at her with his whole arm. "I knew you were part of this. You two whiny snowflakes have been stalking me and breaking into my family's property. You just admitted it." With a flourish, he again brandished his phone. "And I was recording it. Now I've got a confession."

Leah rolled her eyes. "Well, then, you just recorded yourself admitting you took the yearbook supplements, genius. And, guess what." She held up *her* phone. I felt so left out. "I was recording too."

These journalism types: all about the gotcha moment.

Tyler lunged for her phone. Without thinking, I bent my knees, slid one foot forward, and gave him a two-handed snake push, putting all my weight behind it. I guess three years of Little Dragons Junior Kung Fu at the Rec Center had created some serious muscle memory. Even better, it worked—thanks, Sifu Chris!

Tyler went sprawling. Unfortunately, he took me with him. We landed on the tile with a giant clatter and the best I could do was make sure I landed on top and elbow-first. It still hurt, but I was comforted by the thought that it surely hurt Tyler more.

I heard a gasp and looked up to find Mrs. Ritter in the doorway of the yearbook room with an appalled look on her face. "What is going on out here?!"

Leah stepped up. "Tyler fainted and Hal tried to catch him."

Beneath me, Tyler heaved. "Oh my god, *get off me!*" He was giving it his all but I'm nearly five-ten and I'm no underwear model.

Before rolling to the side, I whispered in his ear, "Mutually assured destruction, Tyler. Keep your mouth shut." I made a little kaboom gesture with my hands and Tyler responded with a venomous look.

Mrs. Ritter sent Leah back into the yearbook room to work and insisted on escorting an irate—but silent—Tyler to the nurse's office. As soon as they disappeared around the corner, Leah poked her head back out into the hall.

"What are we going to do?" she hissed.

I peered around her into the yearbook room, where a handful of people labored at Mac stations. "Maybe we should talk about this later."

Leah waved her hand dismissively. "Freshmen." But she came

all the way out into the hallway and closed the door behind her. "Do you think he'll keep his mouth shut?"

"Tyler? No."

"But we have a recording of him admitting to taking the supplements." She held up her phone.

"He can say he was playing along to get us to admit we broke into his house and his brother's building. When he has a little time to think about it, he'll realize this."

"We could say the same thing! It would be his word against ours. Why would anyone believe *Tyler* over us?"

"Because Tyler can prove I was snooping around his house and his brother's building. And I bet he can come up with even more camera footage if he wants to. We, on the other hand, can't prove Tyler took the supplements because we haven't found them."

Leah looked sick. "Oh. Right."

This could not happen right now. Not now that my scholarship plans were finally falling into place. I was already in trouble with the Sheriff's Office for possible unauthorized entry and, oh yeah, the theft of millions of dollars' worth of tacky oil paintings of Venice and diamond-encrusted cat charms. I did not need Tyler Lofaro running around with proof that I had been breaking into places.

"Crap," I said in resignation. "Now we really have to find those supplements."

CHAPTER 16

Of course, we still had no idea where to look next. And neither of us, at present, had time to consider it. Leah went back into the yearbook room and I took off running for my truck. I finished my service calls in record time and made it over to the Sheriff's Office a few minutes early. Grant met me at the door, alone.

"You didn't bring Mike?" I asked in alarm. If you're about to be deported to Guatemala, Grant is your man. But if the residents of Montecito are brandishing their Christofle pitchforks, demanding justice, and the law points its long arm at you, you want a lawyer who knows their way around a jury selection.

"Mike spoke with Inspector Beamish earlier. They've located Irma Campos, and something big must have come up because he's suddenly too busy to talk to you. Probably Irma cleared you. And guess what. I got your phone back." He set my iPhone in my hand with a flourish. I eyed it ambivalently. "They even charged it for you."

Ha. Before Mike had arrived the night before, I'd given Inspector Beamish my passcode. He'd probably searched my phone. I hoped he'd had fun reading eighty thousand text messages from my mom graphically detailing her early pregnancy woes.

"Okay, one of my hearings got moved up." Grant patted me on the shoulder and headed for the parking lot. "Gotta go."

I lifted my phone and, with thumbs stiff from disuse, sent my dad a text telling him not to drive all the way out to the Sheriff's Office. It sounded like Irma had vouched for me so I guessed I wasn't going to jail—not for that, anyway. And I wouldn't have to deal with my dad and Grant in the same building. My day was looking up.

I pulled onto the 101 and headed south in the slow lane. It was almost four-thirty. I wanted to go home. I wanted to pet my dog and make a sandwich and lie in the grass, even if no one but the dog was going to lie in it with me. But one item still loomed large on Hal's Big List of Potential Disasters. Leah and I needed a plan to deal with this Tyler thing. A good plan, which was not exactly our forté, so we needed to get on that. At four-thirty, Leah would still be toiling away in the yearbook room. I sighed as I passed the exit for Carillo Street—and home—and continued on toward school.

My phone pinged with an incoming text as I drove up Garden. Ugh. It was going to take some time to reaccustom myself to my electronic shackles. I waited until I was responsibly parked in the mostly empty parking lot of the high school to check the display. Montana's name was on the lock screen. I swiped.

"Do u have a new phone yet? Need u," her text read.

I dialed and she answered instantly. "Oh, good. You bought a phone."

"Close enough. What's up?"

"Can you meet us at school?"

I glanced out the window. "Sure."

"Okay. Text me when you get here." She hung up.

I pulled the phone away from my ear and texted, "Here."

Two minutes later Montana emerged from the building and stomped over to my truck. I opened the door.

"There you are," she said. "Finally."

"What's up?"

"I cannot deal ANYMORE. These bugs are *so disgusting*." She illustrated her point with a violent shudder.

I'm used to hearing this. People say this to me daily, sometimes multiple times a day (which is a strong indicator my life is currently on a poor trajectory). But this was my best friend talking, so I did my best to look concerned. "What bugs? Why are you still here? I thought you had sailing practice."

"Oh, you know. Sailing didn't work out," she said, sounding very casual all of a sudden. "We joined color guard."

"Okay . . ." That seemed like an abrupt change. I didn't know we had a color guard. I didn't know what color guard even was. "Is color guard like Junior ROTC?"

"No," she answered shortly. "Now, focus. We dress out in the locker rooms in the gym and those bugs I told you about have TAKEN OVER."

"I thought Coach Bell was going to call the pest control guys," I said.

"Yeah, well, they're useless. They came, they sprayed, nothing happened. If anything, it's worse!" She looked at me expectantly.

I felt like a dermatologist at a cocktail party (minus the prestige and fat income). "That doesn't sound good."

"Hal!"

I sighed and climbed out of the truck. "Show me."

Montana strode purposefully toward the gym, towing me along in her wake. Just inside the door, her sister stood waiting under the basketball goal. "She'll take care of it," Montana told her.

Madison turned to face the gym and yelled, "Hal is here! She's going to fix the bugs!" The dozen or so people scattered throughout the gym stopped what they were doing and stared. Montana steamed ahead, her grip on my wrist unbreakable, and Madison fell in behind us.

Coach Bell poked his head out of the weight room as we passed. "What's going on?"

"Hal is going to fix the bug problem," Madison announced.

"Um . . ." I said uncertainly. If the school district guys had been in there, they had probably done the exact same things I would do. Pest control, at its core, is man versus nature and, you know, sometimes nature wins.

"Great. Have at it," Coach Bell said wearily. He looked about as bad as Ms. Grijalva—maybe worse since he had not availed himself of the rejuvenating benefits of eye toner.

Our march continued and by the time we reached the locker rooms, everyone we'd passed along the way had gathered behind us. An athletic-looking woman in her early twenties stood outside the girls locker room wearing yoga pants and a T-shirt emblazoned with a crossed sword and flag and the words: Spin it, Toss it, Catch it. Someone was really going to have to explain to me what a color guard was.

"Is this your bug friend?" she asked Montana. "Awesome!" She turned to Coach Bell. "I cleared the room so you can come in if you want to, Brad."

In the end, everyone came. About twenty people in all crowded into the locker room, huddling back by the door and chattering like NASCAR commentators while I surveyed the scene. Dead bugs, each just slightly bigger than the head of a pin, coated every flat surface. Floors, benches, windowsills—all of them were covered with tiny insect carcasses. It was, to borrow a technical term from my dad, "a whompin' infestation."

"Anyone seen any live ones?" I asked the crowd.

"I've seen few," a girl in the back volunteered. "Mostly around the showers."

"I see live ones on the ceiling during PE," Montana offered. "But then they die and fall on the floor."

Coach Bell made a helpless gesture. "I've been getting maintenance in here every night to clean but the girls say they're always back by first period."

Well, that fit. "These are drugstore beetles," I explained. "They're hard to get rid of unless you get them at the source. They lay their eggs in dry goods, like dried food or dried plants. They can even hatch in papers and packing materials. Is there a storage closet or anything in here?"

Coach Bell and the woman, who I'd brilliantly deduced was the color guard coach, both shook their heads. The woman added, "The custodial closet is down the hall."

Well, goody. I had a nice, big audience here to witness my pest control fail. I gave Montana an apologetic look. "I can spray again if you want, but everyone will need to clear out for at least two hours. And, without spraying the eggs at the source, it probably won't help much."

Montana gave me an exasperated look and lifted her hands, palms up. "So find the source."

I glanced around, at a loss. It was a locker room, there wasn't much to it. Toilet stalls, sinks, lockers, benches, a couple of questionable looking showers . . . "Is there stuff in these lockers?"

Coach Bell shook his head. "No locks allowed. They get used during the PE classes to store extra clothes. That's about it."

"I guess they could come up out of the drains," I said, without much conviction. "I can put some gel down those." Maybe the light fixtures? Montana said she'd seen bugs on the ceiling. No, the fixtures in here were really basic, just housings with long, bare fluorescent bulbs. I couldn't see any place— wait a sec. My gaze snagged on a ripple in one of the foam ceiling tiles, much like the one Leah and I had displaced to launch the Darth Vader car. But it wasn't like anyone could actually store anything up there. The metal framework that supported the tiles was only designed to hold the foam tiles and maybe a couple of light fixtures. Except. The ceiling tiles in this locker room only covered a five-foot-wide strip down the middle of the room, presumably to provide access to plumbing and electrical systems. On either side of that, the ceiling was conventional plaster. It was not the kind of space anyone would use for storage, but all kinds of strange things happened during building construction. I'd once drilled a small hole above the baseboard of a bathroom wall, stuck my dad's camera snake inside, and found a bunch of rotting pizza boxes. The drywallers who'd built that home had thrown their lunch trash between the studs and, when the job was finished, just walled everything up. The rats had been thrilled. The homeowners less so.

I turned to Coach Bell. "Got a flashlight and a ladder?"

The ladder was more of a step stool. I set it by a conveniently located bank of lockers and used it to scramble up on top of them. There I crouched like an osteoporotic frog, my head brushing the ceiling.

"Please don't fall off that," Coach Bell requested. The crowd behind him, which seemed to have grown larger, looked on. Didn't athletes have homework?

I chose the warped tile because there was an enticing, X-marks-the-spot quality to it. Extending my arm blindly (since there wasn't room to look up) I shoved the tile up and out of the way. Instantly a shower of tiny specks rained down. My elementary school earthquake conditioning took over and I assumed the duck-and-cover position just as something larger and harder followed them down.

"Mmmmh," I moaned, mouth tightly closed, as I attempted to retract my neck and head into my torso. There was no escaping the awful reality of it. My hair was completely covered in tiny dead insects. Incidentally, a fair number of them had also fallen down my shirt. Yeah, there were dead bugs in my bra. Yay, me.

"What the hell is this?" The color guard coach exclaimed, her voice throbbing with outrage. "Is this a *camera?*"

Some part of my brain registered that the heavy falling projectile had been a hidden camera. In the girls locker room. The repercussions of that were sure to be interesting. But I was here on a mission. I shook my hair vigorously in a movement my mom would have described as a "head bang" and tried to focus. Moving cautiously, I stretched upward until my head and shoulders poked though the newly created gap in the ceiling tiles. I switched on the flashlight and panned the space, prepared for rotting pizza boxes or, who knew, maybe bodies. This was a high school locker room. It was, like, the perfect place to hide something stinky.

Instead, my flashlight illuminated row after row of tidy-looking cardboard boxes. And, on the side of each, printed in distinctive green lettering, were the words "Greengroup Publishing, Inc."

Holy crap. I'd found the yearbook supplements.

Things moved surprisingly fast after that. I texted Leah. Coach Bell called the assistant principal while the color guard coach breathed fire and ejected the spectators from the locker room.

If Leah and the AP hadn't converged on the locker room within moments of each other, Tyler might have gotten away with everything. After all, there was nothing obvious to tie him to any of it. But Leah, future Pulitzer Prize–winning investigative journalist and erstwhile yearbook editor, had been all over Tyler for months. She had compiled a dossier on Tyler that included, among other things, his Reddit handle. Five minutes on her phone and she was able to produce evidence of someone using that handle to post clips of this locker room. That was enough proof for the AP, who called in the principal and the police.

There was still nothing, short of dusting for fingerprints (which Leah suggested but the AP vetoed on grounds that a) our high school lacked a crime scene investigation unit and b) Tyler, as a member of the yearbook staff, had a perfectly reasonable excuse for having his fingerprints on those boxes) to conclusively connect Tyler to the yearbook supplements, but, based on everyone's reaction to the camera thing, no additional proof would be necessary. Tyler was on his way to expulsion and possibly arrest. Leah was a hero.

I assisted in the removal of ten bug-infested boxes of yearbook supplements from the rafters and sprayed the area thoroughly. Then I went home.

CHAPTER 17

One week later, things had calmed down considerably. The bug population of the girls locker room had fallen to normal numbers. Tyler was suspended, though he had yet to face charges and his parents were appealing the suspension. Montana and Madison seemed to be enjoying color guard, and I had settled into a steady routine of school, work, study, repeat.

According to local papers, the Santa Barbara Sheriff's Office had contacted the owners of the rat estate in Montecito, who were currently in residence at their Sagaponack home and unaware of the presence of any guests at their Santa Barbara property. They provided department investigators with Irma's info and the Sheriff's deputies, succeeding where I'd failed, had tracked Irma to an address in Lompoc. She was arrested and, after questioning, provided investigators with the identities of The Guests. As it turned out, the masterminds behind the theft of millions of dollars of overpriced status symbols, the notorious "Estate Bandits," were two Instagram-famous practitioners of natural homeopathic medicine from Calabasas. No one was surprised.

From my perspective, it was situation normal. No frantic imperative to develop interests I didn't have. No awful white van. No trespassing. And no shirtless neighbor boy dropping into my backyard.

This last one bothered me.

So, early Friday evening, I stood in front of the full-length mirror in my bedroom and gave myself a once-over.

Hair: slicked back into fancy(-ish) ponytail.

Face: expertly made-up by Madison, remaining bruises covered.

Dress: short and black.

Shoes: beaded ballet flats. Yeah, flats. I mean, let's be real. There are limits.

Reasonably satisfied, I exited through the slider, walked across the lawn to the dock box, hoisted myself up on top of the wall, and dropped onto the grass on the other side. Smoothing my skirt back into place, I turned to find Spencer on the pool chaise, watching me with wide eyes.

Eep.

I had expected him to be in the house at this hour. Or even at the Homecoming dance. I'd been prepared for that too. It wasn't like I'd expected him to sit at home waiting on me or anything. God. I cringed imagining the view he'd gotten as I'd shimmied over the wall. And now the little speech I'd prepared for when/if he came to answer the door would sound ridiculous. I would have to wing it.

"You still want to go to homecoming?" I blurted. What can I say? Winging it never works out well for me.

Spencer's eyebrows were still up around his hairline. "After that, I think I'd say yes to anything you asked me." I felt myself blushing but I was reasonably certain the industrial grade spackle Madison had troweled on my face would conceal it.

"I know I should say no," he continued, "as a matter of principle. But I'm not feeling very principled right now."

"You are entitled to your principles," I said formally, sounding like the chairman from *Iron Chef*. I wanted to smack myself on the forehead. This is why I'd *prepared* a speech. I so hated talking. Well, there was nothing for it. I'd have to soldier on. "As it happens, I agree with your principles. I get it. I'm hoping you'll give me a chance to show you I get it."

Spencer studied me intently. "Okay," he said at last. "Let's go."

We stared at each other a moment longer until I broke the silence. "You'll need a shirt," I told him.

Spencer went into his house and emerged ten minutes later dressed very conventionally in khaki slacks, a white collared shirt, and a well-tailored navy blazer. On his feet he wore slip-on Seavees. Like I said, there are limits.

He looked amazing.

With a courtly gesture, he motioned toward the wall. I gave him an evil look and led the way down his driveway, through the gate, and around to my front yard. I'd forgotten to bring my keys so I ducked into my house, surprising my dad as he sat on the couch watching mixed martial arts. He turned to say something and froze, his face rigid with shock. "Why do you look like that?" he asked, sounding appalled.

Spencer stuck his head in the front door. "Hi, Mr. Mayhew."

My dad recoiled, almost falling off the couch. "You're going out? With him? Wearing *that*?"

I handed Spencer the envelope with the Homecoming tickets to put in his pocket. Spencer gave my dad a cheeky grin. "Don't worry. I promised my parents she wouldn't keep me out too late."

Rolling my eyes, I grabbed his arm and dragged him outside, pulling the door closed behind me.

The Homecoming dance is always held in the Meadow, which is what everyone calls our sports field. The name fits. It's more like a lush, sylvan glade that is sometimes accessorized with lacrosse goals than a conventional field. I parked the truck in the lot and Spencer and I followed the sounds of live music down the hill. The hedges on either side had been draped with white fairy lights. Down on the Meadow, more fairy lights had been strung between posts, delineating a large area for the festivities. Paper lanterns in school colors dangled amongst the lights. A band played on a raised wooden platform while our fellow students chatted and danced on the portable dance floor and generally acted much more civilized than usual. It was lovely.

And there wasn't a speck of glitter anywhere, so I didn't see why they couldn't have let me help.

As she approached with Madison, I shot Montana an irritated look, which she ignored. "Okay," she announced. "We're all set. Madison will go up to Coach Presley and do her thing. When Coach Presley steps away from the beverage table, I'll track down Coach Bell and tell him he has to go back to his original station."

"There's a rule that two adults have to be monitoring the drinks at all times," Madison explained to Spencer, who was looking confused.

Montana turned to me. "Hal, your job is to prepare Ms. G. for the switch. Gently. Make sure she doesn't run away."

"I'm on it."

"What is going on?" Spencer broke in, frowning at me. "I thought we were going to dance."

"I told you I was going to show you I understood why I upset you. How would I do that with dancing?"

Montana gave a businesslike clap. "Great, let's do this." She and Madison strolled away.

Spencer was not looking thrilled, but he didn't leave, either.

We watched as Madison dashed over to the refreshment table—an impressive feat in five-inch heels—and came to a stumbling, breathless halt just in front of the color guard coach.

Spencer asked, "What is she going to . . . oh."

When a group of friends grows from infancy to adolescence within two hundred feet of each other, they are inevitably around to witness each other's developmental hiccups. Relevant to that moment was the summer Madison had turned four. None of us would forget that summer because that was when Madison had exchanged her marathon temper-tantrums for a more unique method of channeling frustration. Instead of throwing herself onto the ground and screaming and maybe bonking her head against the floor for added emphasis, she'd learned to vent her feelings using her big girl words. At first, the adults in her life had encouraged this. Unfortunately, Madison being Madison, her big girl words had come out so quickly she'd been unintelligible. This had only added to her frustration and she would talk faster and faster, growing more and more excited, until at last she hyperventilated and passed out. Mrs. Forbes had sent her to several therapists to work on this and, eventually, she'd stopped. Mostly.

Her sister and I were the only people aware that she maintained the ability to do this on command. And maybe Spencer. If he hadn't known before, he certainly did now.

We waited nearby as Madison worked her magic. Coach Presley stood, visibly alarmed, as Madison motormouthed her way to an agitated collapse. Seconds before the faint, Madison lifted the back of her hand to her forehead in a move so phony I thought the gig was up, but I guess she looked unsteady enough to sell it because Coach Presley turned to Ms. Grijalva, muttered a few urgent words, and led/carried Madison from the Meadow.

"That's our cue," I told Spencer, already moving.

Ms. Grijalva stood behind one of four open punch bowls, looking nervous. We halted in front of her and I announced, "Don't worry. Reinforcements are on their way."

"Oh, good," she said, visibly relieved. "I don't know why they can't put the punch in some of those glass beverage dispensers. They look nice and they have *lids*."

I nodded but my attention was on the dance floor as I kept an eye out for Montana. When I saw her moving our way, herding a reluctant-looking Coach Bell in front of her, I turned to Ms. Grijalva, thinking hard. I needed her to spill her guts. I needed her to repeat to Coach Bell everything she'd confided to me—ideally with a little extra contrition and some smoochy stuff thrown in. I had to do this just right or she would freak out and say nothing or, worse, run away before he got here.

"Ms. Grijalva." I met her eyes and gave her a bolstering smile. "Coach Bell is on his way over here. This is your chance. Don't blow it."

Beside me, Spencer shook his head.

"Wha?" She clutched the edge of the table. Her knuckles turned white. Too late for escape! Montana deposited Coach Bell behind a row of two-liter drink bottles and stepped back to observe. She shot me an inquiring glance, which I answered with a thumbs-up. Spencer rolled his eyes.

Ms. Grijalva let go of the table. "Brad," she said hesitantly.

Coach Bell gave a brusque nod, his eyes on the band.

She took a step closer. "Brad, please." She let out a long, ragged sigh. "Okay, I know you're mad. You have every right. I was so insensitive. And I've missed you, *so* much—but I completely understand if you never want to have anything to do with me ever again. Like, I get it. But I can't live with . . . with you thinking that I don't believe you're good enough. That's not true. *At all.* I'm not saying you were wrong. You weren't. All I was thinking about was what my sisters would say and, honestly, who cares what they say? They're jerks. This—you're great—this was never about you. This was about me, and how I have to learn to be my own person, and be confident in my own decisions. And I don't blame you for a second for not wanting to be part of that process. It's not your problem. But it's important to me that you know that you're *awesome* and I am thankful for every day I had with you." She picked up a Chinet cup of what looked like Sprite and gulped it down. "Okay, you can ignore me now."

Coach Bell turned to her, brows lowered, and met her gaze for long, agonizing seconds. "I'm not an idiot," he said forcefully.

Ms. Grijalva responded passionately, "You're the best man I've ever met." Which wasn't exactly agreement.

He turned to Spencer. "You kids can watch the drink table, right?"

"Yeah," Spencer said, sounding resigned.

Coach Bell took Ms. Grijalva by the hand and led her off into the night.

I held up a bottle of iced tea in one hand and a fizzy lemonade in the other. "Arnold Palmer?"

Spencer waited for me to take a seat on the chaise, then dropped down beside me. It was a very nice chaise, with striped cushions made of thick, closed-cell foam. I barely felt his landing.

"Well that was . . . different," he remarked.

The dance was long over. We'd stayed after to help pack up

the fairy lights and leftover soft drinks. I'd driven us back to my house and escorted Spencer home. Well, home to his yard, anyway. And, as usual, we'd ended up by the pool.

"Yeah," I began, aware the events of the evening may not have made my point as well as I'd hoped. Feeling the need to elaborate, I turned to Spencer. "So, about what I said to you. I was focused on certain things, and didn't pay much attention to other things, and I got those other things wrong." Oh, wow, gee, wasn't that articulate? I let out a frustrated breath and pushed myself up off of the chaise. "Forget it."

Spencer laughed and grabbed my arm, pulling me back down. "No, no, hold on. Hal, seriously. Wait a sec. I think I get the point you were trying to make, watching all that between Coach Bell and Ms. Grijalva. But I object to the analogy. *I'm* really *not* an idiot."

I covered my face with my hand. "I know. That didn't go like I'd imagined. I wanted you to see that I understand why you're angry, that I understand I was, I dunno . . . distracted, or self-absorbed . . . and made a lot of stupid assumptions about you. I mean, look at you right now: wearing a shirt. A shirt with buttons, even. I was wrong about literally everything."

Spencer's expression registered a hint of embarrassment. "Actually, you were right about the shirts. I have a thing about shirts. You probably don't remember, when I was about three I was diagnosed with a sensory processing disorder. I outgrew it, but with shirts—the tags still bother me."

I wanted to hide in shame, but there was no way I'd fit under the chaise. "Oh my god. I was *not* right. I'm an even bigger jerk than I realized." I stood. "I'm gonna go home now."

Spencer reached out and caught my hand. His hand was dry and very warm. "I just wanted you to pay attention to me."

I met his gaze. "I'm paying attention now. If you still want me to."

His mouth stretched in a slow grin. "Want to go for a swim?"

That sounded promising. He was being awfully forgiving, here. A swim seemed like the least I could do. I glanced down at the clear, moonlit water. "It's not too late? It's kind of chilly."

Spencer stood and closed the distance between us. "The heater's on. It's nice and warm."

I stepped in even closer, smelling the fresh scent of his shampoo. Or maybe it was his shaving cream. I was seized with a bizarre urge to sniff his neck. "Sounds good," I murmured absently.

He moved all the way into my space. "If you get hungry later, I can make waffles."

"Oh, perfect." I looked up and we locked eyes.

Spencer trailed his hand down my bare arm and dropped his forehead to mine. "Should I walk with you to get your suit?"

I'd parted my lips—to agree!—when Mr. Salazar appeared, backlit, in the kitchen doorway and squinted into the night. "Hey, Spencer?"

I jumped back, away from Spencer. The smooth sole of my ballet flat hit the edge of the pool coping and slid. Spencer used his hold on my arm to arrest my fall and held firm while I found my footing. "Right here," he called.

"Ah." Mr. Salazar came down the steps and crossed the lawn, halting a few feet away. He studied us for a moment, his expression amused, then held out a folded sheet of letterhead to Spencer. "This came in the mail. It's from the Verhaag Scholarship Committee."

I froze. Did that mean mine had come too? Surely they sent all the notices out at once. I needed to excuse myself right away and go check my mailbox—

Spencer's dad continued, "I was going to let you open it but your mom found it first. I've got to warn you, she's not very happy right now. Thanksgiving is going to be pure hell."

Spencer walked over to the post by the outdoor shower and flipped a switch. The underwater pool lights came on, illuminating the pool deck in a wavering, aqua glow. He returned and took the letter from his father, unfolding it briskly. His face paled. His expression turned grim. I felt a twinge of conscience. Sure, he claimed otherwise but . . . had Spencer secretly hoped to win? He'd written a poem, though. I was sure Spencer was a very capable poet but a narrative poem influenced by Robert W. Service, structured *exactly* like his works? He'd had no hope of winning with something like that. Still, it had to be hard having a famous novelist for a father. Poor Spencer.

Spencer looked up and met my eyes. "Hal," he rubbed his jaw nervously, looking a little ill. I waited for him to say more. The silence stretched.

Mr. Salazar's eyes moved back and forth between the two of us. Abruptly, he turned on his heel and headed back to the house, a strange look on his face.

"What is it, Spencer?" I was dying to get out of here and check my own mailbox.

Spencer extended his arm and offered me the letter. Impatiently, I took it and scanned the opening lines.

Dear Mr. Salazar,

On behalf of this year's Verhaag Scholarship Committee, congratulations!

I re-read that sentence a few more times. My chest burned. My head felt light. Hands trembling, I folded the letter with deliberate care and passed it back to Spencer. Then I turned to go.

He reached for my arm. "Hal, wait."

I reacted instinctively, shoving my elbow back as hard as I could. Spencer's response was an "*oof*" followed by a very satisfying splash.

I walked myself home.

News Digest for September 30

Santa Barbara News-Journal

VERHAAG SCHOLARSHIP WINNER ANNOUNCED

For the eighth time in the history of the prestigious bequest, the Verhaag Scholarship has been awarded to a direct descendant of Augusta Verhaag. Spencer Salazar, son of bestselling novelist Oscar Salazar and Olivia Salazar (neé Verhaag), was one of two Verhaag family members competing for this year's award. The scholarship includes full tuition to the college or university of the winner's choice. This year's runner-up, Hallie Mayhew, received a twenty-five-dollar gift card to Starbucks.

Mitchell Putnam, Commodore of the Santa Barbara Yacht Club and spokesman for this year's panel of judges, said in a statement, "We are pleased to award this year's Verhaag Scholarship to Spencer Salazar. We all greatly enjoyed Spencer's poem and expect he will produce many more works of fine verse in the years to come."

Previous winners of the Verhaag Scholarship have all submitted research papers exploring the work of famed Gold Rush–era poet Robert W. Service. This is the first time the Verhaag Scholarship has been awarded to the writer of a narrative poem. With permission from Mr. Salazar, we have reprinted his winning composition below.

The Shooting of Bat McPoo by Spencer Salazar, writing as "Dis Service"

There's things been done 'neath th' tropic sun that might seem
  strange to newbies;
But it's paradise for frigate birds an' herring gulls an' boobies;
An' where you find the avian kind you'll find guano hunters, too,
An' whither they sails, they carries the tales of Bigamous Bat McPoo.
His story's queer but it's good to hear, if wisdom is what you seek,
An' I'd love to regale what I know of the tale, but my throat is too
  dry to speak . . .

So I bought him a drink, then I bought him a few, then the night
  became kind of a blur;
An' I think that these are my notes below but who can be really
  sure . . . ?

A loud local crowd held a wedding reception at the El Crab
  Catcher Saloon;
An' a ukulele an' a steel guitar serenaded the Waikiki moon;
An' the guano men all had their finery on an' their socks was
  turned inside out,
An' all the eligible girls in town was workin' their "come hither"
  pout.
An' the bride holding court at the end of the bar was the lady they
  called Mayhew,
An' at her beck and call stood the greatest of all of the guano
  men, Bat McPoo.

Now there's fortune 'n' fame in the guano game for them that
    knows howta play;
But for each guano hunter who strikes it rich there's ten thousand
    that washes away;
An' ten thousand families out in the street or sweethearts alone
    in their beds,
Victims of lust for guano which blinds men's eyes and plays dirty
    tricks on their heads.
But Bat McPoo's luck was true and he always found where th'
    richest and best poo be—
When we asked him his trick, he gave his eyelash a flick and said
    "You want guano,
follow th' boobies."

So Bat McPoo had struck it rich an' sold out an' headed home,
But changing planes in Honolulu he stopped to buy a comb.
An' t'was there he met his heart's true love, the lady they called
    Mayhew;
An' he bought her a penthouse in Sheraton Towers, as newlyweds
    sometimes will do;
An' they settled in to their new condo life to live happily evermore,
An' forgot all about any woes in the pasts they each had lived
    before.

When out of the night, which was balmy and sweet and into the
    genteel atmosphere,
came a smokin' wahine in a fishnet top, with a poinsettia pinned
    by her ear.
She looked like a girl who could handle herself and never be
    bothered with money,

But she tossed her Amex card at the barkeep and purred, "Next
round's on me, honey . . . ."
There was none could place th' woman's face, though we searched
ourselves for a clue,
But we drank to her health, and the one who drank deepest was
baleful Bat McPoo.

There's women that somehow make you wanna hold them hard
for a spell,
'Til desire becomes so great you'd happily sell yer soul in hell.
She had legs for days and the laughing gaze of a girl who's even
younger,
As she nibbled th' salt on the rim of her glass with sublimated
hunger.
An' I got to thinking who she was, and wondering what she'd do,
An' I turned my head and saw watching her, the lady that's called
Mayhew.

So up an' down th' bar th' ladies toasted to Ms. Mayhew,
An' th' wonderful luck that had brought her to her heartlight,
Bat McPoo.
An' they wished her happiness all through 'er life, an' never a
reason to frown,
An' th' steel guitar bloke went out for a smoke an' the ukulele kid
set his ax down.
An' th' strange woman picked up the ukulele an' strummed a few
chords on th' thing;
Then she closed her eyes and opened her lips—my God! but that
woman could sing.

Have you ever been out on th' Midway Reach when the moon
    was awful 'n' clear,
An' the mighty peaks of the ocean swells can fill yer heart
    with fear;
With only some jerky or oatmeal or beans and a six-pack or two
    of Hinano,
A half dead thing in a deep blue world, enslaved by your lust for
    guano;
While on some nearby nameless and uncharted rock gathered
    ten thousand square miles
of birds?—
Then you understand what her music evoked . . . isolation and
    mountains of turds.

An' isolation that's not the casual kind, that's cured by an evening
    with friends,
But the isolation a woman feels who falls for the wrong kinda men;
Who've learnt ya can't keep a tidy home with an oaf passed out
    on the floor;
Who only wanted what all girls want but wishes she'd held out
    for more,
Who's found herself joined at the hip to a brute and wondering
    what she should do—
An' I saw comprehension spread over the face of the lady they
    called Mayhew.

Then the music changed and grew suddenly soft, so soft that you
    scarce could hear;
And it made you feel like someone you trusted just shoved a
    sharp stick up your rear;

That someone had broken their sacred word, and that all your
  love was a joke;
Your hopes were void, your life destroyed, and your future gone
  up in smoke.
The cry of love in unbearable grief that has curled up and died
  on the floor—
"I could use some fresh air," mumbled Bat McPoo, an' sidled off
  toward the door.

An' the singing faded and died away . . . then exploded back with
  a crash;
An' she seemed to say, "You can run away, but I'm keeping half
  the cash."
An' th' sense was evoked of a promise broke, like it was only
  yesterday,
An' th' steel guitar's whine shrieked, "Vengeance is mine!" then
  the music died away . . .
An' the wahine looked 'round and she batted her eyes, which
  shone from the strength of
her grievin';
An' 'er lips pooched out in a kind of pout, and she spoke and her
  voice was even;
An' she said, "I'm a girl who gets what she wants," and we all saw
  the gun that she
drew,
"An' there's only two things in the world I want now . . . an' they're
  swingin' from Bat
McPoo!"

Then they turned up the lights (it was quarter to two) and
　　everyone looked round the
floor,
An' it then became clear that McPoo wasn't here an' we heard
　　somethin' out the side door.
Then McPoo came walkin' in, backward an' shakin', completely
　　abandoned of grace,
And we saw that the lady they called Mayhew had her navy colt
　　pointed straight at 'is face.
Then the lights went out, then the thunder of guns, and then all
　　the lights came back on,
And McPoo was dead with "two in the head" and both of the
　　women were gone.
An' they've never neither been seen again but the guano men
　　tell tales;
Of an uncharted rock on the Midway Reach where weary men
　　furl their sails;
Of beautiful women and great clouds of boobies beyond reefs
　　that'll send ya to Dave's,
Whose voices call to them so lonely an' sweet, grown men throw
　　themselves into the
waves.
An' they say when the sun's sinkin' low in th' west an' th' sky is
　　aflame in its glory,
Through the cries of the boobies, they hear sirens singing . . . But
　　that's another lo-o-ng
story.

Santa Barbara Independent

ANN COULTER FILES LAWSUIT AGAINST SANTA BARBARA YACHT CLUB

Polarizing author and television personality Ann Coulter has filed suit against Santa Barbara Yacht Club, alleging they bear financial responsibility for damages sustained by her boat in Santa Barbara Harbor earlier this month. Witnesses to the incident reported seeing a small sailing dinghy owned by the Santa Barbara Yacht Club Junior Sailing Program ram Coulter's seventy-foot Sea Ray motor yacht, dislodging her custom fiberglass sunbathing platform and causing it to sink to the bottom of the harbor.

Coulter's attorney states the lawsuit is being filed after Coulter and the yacht club failed to reach a settlement. Santa Barbara Yacht Club Commodore Mitchell Putnam, who rose to his position just days after the incident occurred, declined to comment. No video footage of the collision exists and the skipper of the dinghy has not been identified.

"I was deliberately targeted for my views," Ms. Coulter told reporters in a Wednesday press conference. "I stand up for the forgotten, hard-working Americans who have no voice, and coastal elites respond by vandalizing my yacht." Ms. Coulter added that the unknown teenage skipper responsible for the damage was "probably an illegal."

Montecito Times

10,000 DOLLAR REWARD GIVEN TO LOCAL HERO
FOR ASSISTING IN CAPTURE OF ESTATE BANDITS

In a special ceremony held at the Montecito Country Club on Wednesday, Santa Barbara Mayor Alice Gardiner awarded a check for ten-thousand dollars to the resident who aided in the capture and arrest of the Estate Bandits, a three-person crime syndicate responsible for the theft of over 4.5 million dollars' worth of valuables from Montecito homes. Misty Bottleton-Banks, who flew in from St. Barth's for the occasion, provided Sheriff's deputies with the name and address of her house manager, a woman who was later revealed to be one of the thieves.

In her acceptance speech, Mrs. Bottleton-Banks announced her intention to donate the reward money to Santa Barbara Polo Pony Rescue.

EPILOGUE

One month later

I trudged out the front door at six-fifteen, as usual. The sun was just rising above the bluff. The palm trees were gray silhouettes against the pink dawn sky and the mountains were dark in the distance. The wet of the cold, dewy grass soaked through my Vans, but I didn't hurry. There was no need to worry about being tardy to first period these days; Ms. Grijalva had been strolling in later than ever, her heart full and her beverage decaffeinated. She was dopey in love and I was happy for her. Really.

As usual, Bluff Drive was deserted at this hour. My dad had left for work fifteen minutes ago. A month earlier, I would have gone with him in hopes of squeezing in an extra billable hour. Now there was no point. Without the Verhaag Scholarship, Georgetown was comically out of reach. Damp, salty air tickled my nose and I paused in the driveway to zip my hoodie.

I glanced at the hood of my truck, where the box of waffles always waited for me. Spencer had started leaving them for me the morning after the scholarship announcement. He was an early riser and he delivered them every morning as he headed out for his dawn surf sesh. I knew from experience the waffles would still be crispy, the little plastic cup of syrup hot and fragrant.

That first morning, I'd snatched up the box and marched it straight over to the outside trashcan. The nerve of him, thinking I could be bought with waffles. I'd righteously dropped it into the can, where it had landed with a satisfying *foonf*. It had been exactly the response his weak gesture of apology deserved.

But, the next morning, there was another box. I'd gotten a Tupperware from inside the house and transferred the waffles before throwing the box away. An empty box looked just like a full box in the bottom of the trashcan, after all. I was still mad at Spencer but the waffles were innocent. Every day that followed, we'd repeated this process. Spencer had never missed a morning.

Today, though, the hood of my truck stood empty. No waffles.

Well. Good. He'd finally gotten the message. My chest felt heavy. It was probably just hunger. My stomach was all spoiled from the parade of easy breakfast pickings. It would adjust.

I heard something behind me and spun around. Spencer stood there, his wetsuit peeled to his waist, arms crossed over his bare chest. His dark hair stood up on one side where he'd slept on it. Ugh. Even his bedhead looked good.

"Decided to quit wasting your waffles?" I asked, my tone deliberately bored.

Spencer's gray eyes regarded me with cautious determination. "I know you've been eating them."

So much for my Tupperware switcharoo. Hallie Mayhew: Master of Subterfuge. I shrugged. "Yeah, I've been eating your traitor waffles. I can't throw away perfectly good waffles. I'm not a monster."

He prowled closer. "It's been a month. If you want your waffles, you and I are going to have to come to terms."

I stabbed my finger at him. "You screwed me over."

"Not on purpose," he said, his gaze steady.

Okay, maybe it wasn't entirely Spencer's fault the panel of replacement judges had been a bunch of salty old sailing cronies who'd thought his poem was the best thing since nickel beer night. Maybe I was being unreasonable. Well, so what? I was tired of being reasonable. After all I'd put up with, I'd earned the right to be unreasonable. It was *my turn*.

"Fine," I said. "Keep your stupid waffles."

"Hal." He took another step. His voice softened. "I'm sorry."

"You don't get to be sorry. I *needed* that scholarship, Spencer. Do you know what I did yesterday? I pulled a dead raccoon out of an irrigation well. It had been in there a. Long. Time. I'll never unsee that. Then the homeowner screamed at me and called me stupid because I parked in her driveway while I loaded up the raccoon carcass and she couldn't get by in her G-Wagen. Then my mom called and—"

He produced a thick, blue folder and held it out to me. I blinked. I hadn't noticed him holding anything. How did he *do* that? I took the folder and opened it. "What is this?"

"Tall Clubs International Scholarship," said the first page, "Awarding scholarships to people who meet minimum height requirements (178 cm for women, 188 cm for men)." I flipped the top half of the page forward and scanned the one behind it. "American Board of Funeral Service Education National Scholarship Program." Yikes. I pulled both pages out and transferred them to the opposite pocket. The one under those read, "National Potato Council Scholarship." Sure, why not? I moved that to the other pocket, as well. The next page was printed on paper so glossy I had to squint to read it. "*Teen Vogue* Cutest Prom Couple Scholarship Contest. Win $10,000. Are you and your snackie sweetie so adorbs?!" Beside this, Spencer had written YES in emphatic black Sharpie.

I gave a short laugh and ran my thumb along the edge of the stack. There were at least fifty pages here. Fifty different scholarships. It must have taken him ages to come up with all of them.

I looked up and Spencer was suddenly very close. I smelled neoprene and deodorant and boy, and I could see the beginnings of dark stubble on his tan cheeks. I huffed out a long breath. Even I wasn't sure if it was a sigh of forgiveness or defeat. I shook my head. Spencer's shoulders relaxed.

"And you think I could win one of these?" I asked.

Spencer smiled. "I think you could win all of these."

"Not if you help," I told him.

He grabbed my upper arms and jerked me forward. My chest bumped his, the folder flattened between us. Spencer leaned in and put his mouth on mine.

He tasted like hot maple syrup.

ACKNOWLEDGMENTS

Endless thanks to Jason Gagne who, in addition to being the best writing buddy ever, single-handedly developed the Plotpins app, which makes writing so easy it feels like cheating; and to Jennifer Gagne, who held my irascible baby for countless afternoons while Jason and I spitballed. Thanks to Patrick Weaver for composing a poem so brilliant and esoteric, I had no choice but to write a book around it. Thanks to everyone on the Turner team, for making *PEST* happen, and thanks particularly to Stephanie Beard, for loving Bat McPoo as much as I do. Thanks to Elizabeth Kaplan and Timothy Woodward for reading the early draft of *PEST* and sharing their excellent advice. Thanks to expert dance team consultant Idonnarose Ellis and expert pest control consultant Shane Taylor (who inspired so much of this book). Thanks to the family, friends and friends-of-friends who've been so generous with their time, advice, and encouragement: Mary and Hank Foscue, Chris and Ron Sauer, Rae Castroll, Gaby and Emily Gomez, Erika Romer, Nicole Sclama, Zach Dean, Derby and Trevor White, Barry Kemp, RJ Cooper, Melissa Tokstad, Angela Mitchell, and Khristine Serbin. Thanks to Nicole Biergiel and Aaron Laferriere for the good times on *Coconut*. Thanks to Heather Poet-Johnson for her endless—and I do mean *endless*—support. And thanks to the best of the best, Bryan Boyd, who's always making my dreams come true.

ABOUT THE AUTHOR

Elizabeth Foscue grew up in northwest Florida and the British Virgin Islands. She attended the University of Florida, where she majored in Linguistics and fleeing town on football weekends. She met her (now) husband at a sailing team meeting the second week of school and it was his idea to move to Annapolis, Maryland. She earned a J.D. and LL.M. from Georgetown University Law Center before escaping to SoCal after ten years of nasty, mid-Atlantic weather. Elizabeth lives in Santa Barbara, California with her husband, norrbottenspets (that's Swedish for "barking fur-factory") and two awesome kiddos.

CPSIA information can be obtained
at www.ICGtesting.com
Printed in the USA
BVHW031552210322
632013BV00001B/1